THE
CRIMPER
OF
OLD TOWN

LOADED IMAGE
ENTERTAINMENT

First printing edition: February 2020

Cover designed by Jelena Gajic @coverbookdesigns

Published by Loaded Image Entertainment, LLC.

www.loadedimageentertainment.com

THE CRIMPER OF OLD TOWN

Part One of the Novella Series

Written by A.J. Gordon

Edwin's illustrations by Savannah Kay Gordon

BE THE WIND, NOT THE SAIL

Table of Contents

THE CRIMPER OF OLD TOWN

1

GOOD THINGS TO COME

Boston, Massachusetts 1872…A bleak autumn rain pummeled the industrial cobblestone streets of the harbor district, kicked around by frigid winds blowing in from the ocean between wooden buildings that groaned against it to prove their strength. The sun had yet to show itself—not that the sun could have been seen through the impenetrable marine fog looming across the rooftops. Store banners flailed wildly, stretching the limits of the mounting ropes at their corners. An especially worn banner finally had enough and broke free on one side, flapping violently at the wind's whim. Its brass mounts smacked against the second-story window with an absolute disdain for whoever might be inside.

Dwelling within that weathered building on the corner of Summer Street and Kingston, in a loft above his flimsy boot-repair shop, was Edwin Morris Junior—a tall, slender man of nearly twenty-two years old with a laborer's physique and sharp facial features. Now the sole proprietor of Morris Shoemaking Company, he hid his boyish face behind thick, wavy brown hair and a proud mustache in an effort to appear older. Edwin was asleep on a worn hay-stuffed bedroll smashed against a cot that nearly filled the sparse office-turned-domicile he called home. A small wooden desk holding a glass lantern sat nearby, next to a cast-iron stove that took up the rest of the room. The walls were filled, too, with charcoal and graphite drawings done on newssheets tacked haphazardly all around.

Edwin had only been asleep for a few hours, having worked late into the night to meet the deadline of a large order. He woke sluggishly as the banner mount tapped and scraped against the window, a swelling insult. Edwin muttered and rubbed the last bit of sleep from his eyes while hopping up in his mismatched wool pajamas to throw on a pair of sturdy boots and a tattered frock coat picked out from a footlocker at the end of the bed. He yawned, stretched, and shuddered at the relentless tapping outside, further displeased by the sordid weather causing this whole aggravation. "It's not even fucking light out…" Edwin snarled, slicking his hair back and covering it with a soft-crowned hat, singed on one side from leaving it atop the stove vent too long a time or two while cooking.

Edwin plodded down rickety stairs through the dark, too pissed, bitter, and cold to bother igniting a lantern. The shop was a loosely organized mess of tools, manuals, and boot-repair projects in different stages of being finished, all spread across wooden benches that had seen better days. He grabbed pliers and fasteners from a cluttered cabinet against the back wall and shoved everything into his coat pockets, preparing himself to brave the mess outside.

The heavy breeze blew Edwin's hat back as he stepped out, and he barely hung on to it as he tried to shut the shop door behind him. Wrestling with the door's squeaky, uneven hinges, he mashed it back in place as the cold rain pelted his back. *Not even the Canal Street bakers would be up this fucking early*, Edwin thought, disdainfully looking up at the shop's banner flapping wildly in the chaos of wind and rain beating it to death. It was another cutting reminder of how he'd let the family business slide downhill since his father had passed away and left him everything to ruin.

Edwin tightened the hug of his coat and popped the collar up as he made his way around the building to fetch a ladder, which was as weathered as the front door and seemed as if it could break right in half. He climbed up, carefully maintaining his balance while wrestling the banner back into position. Edwin finally got the new mount on to the wet cord and re-attached it to the post, as he had done scores of times before. The fabric showed its age up close. The print was fading, and once-small holes were getting bigger, but its tattered corners were again hooked in securely. Despite himself, Edwin took a moment of pride in the completed work before hopping back down and stowing the ladder.

Back upstairs, Edwin built a small fire in the stove's base. He was soaking wet but too cold to remove his hat or jacket, and it was now too late to go back to bed. He warmed his hands by the crackling fire, pondering the reduction of his circumstances. When Edwin Morris Sr. owned and operated the Morris Shoemaking Company, the building's fixtures were always newfangled and well kept. The loft housed a proper office, and the shop floor was at all times organized and tidy. Business was good, and in addition to Edwin Jr., Edwin Sr. employed an apprentice to help keep up with the workload. Now, the only proof that the upstairs loft had been an office was a rotting desk stuffed into a corner. What had been his father's proudly modest workspace now served as Edwin's food prep counter and closet catchall—when it wasn't covered in the graphite and charcoal drawings that took up much of Edwin's time and made him no money. There had once been a matching chair to the desk as well, but Edwin sacrificed it for stove wood one particularly bad winter night last year.

Edwin never knew his mother. She died giving birth to him, and his father seemed to resent him for it until his own death from pneumonia. He had left Edwin in charge of the business he had grown up wanting nothing to do with, and that first year was turbulent. In order to pay off the shop's newly billowing debts, Edwin sold the family's small cottage outside of town to an unscrupulous land developer below market price. Soon after that, to make ends meet, Edwin let his father's longtime apprentice go, in effect forcing him to open a competing shop a few blocks over that Edwin frequently lost business to. Nevertheless, in the three years since his father's death, business had remained consistent enough for him to eke out a meager survival.

Edwin slammed shut the cast-iron gate of the stove, coming to terms with the long day ahead. He filled a percolator with water from a ceramic jug and set it on the warming stovetop, then reached into his pantry—a small wooden box on the floor—for a fistful of coffee grinds to brew. *It's supposed to be a good day, goddamn it*, he thought, leaning back to roll a cigarette. He was impatient. Not only was he to collect final payment for the job he was delivering on later, at the end of it all, he would get to spend the evening with Lillian, his inamorata. He was to attend an anniversary party and feast at her family's lavish home in South Boston, much to the irritation of Lillian's father, Herman Wilkinson, who was hosting the event with her mother, Marie.

Edwin and Lillian were wholly in love and soon to be married. It would be a summer wedding, and Lillian was the only part of Edwin's life that he felt any excitement for. They'd fallen for each other over the course of a seven-month courtship, no matter how many walls Mr. Wilkinson tried putting up between them. In a recent signal of accepting defeat, Mr. Wilkinson begrudgingly decreed that, once married to Lillian, Edwin would be employed within the successful trading company he had built and put his good family name on. Edwin presumed Mr. Wilkinson made the offer solely to save face with his peers and avoid the shame of having a low-class, shoe-cobbling son-in-law, but Edwin didn't mind. He desperately wanted to escape the slum trappings of his bottom-shelf life through hard work and admirable means, but he was also willing to accept someone giving it to him.

All that really mattered to Edwin was having a profession that would make Lillian proud. Owning a crumbling boot-repair shop in a horseshit-smeared part of town certainly wasn't an option forever. So, even though it would be by passive-aggressive charity at first, Edwin was sure he could prove himself useful within the company over time. It would be a job with a respectful title, important duties, and a salary that could provide the quality of life Mr. Wilkinson felt his only daughter was entitled to.

Edwin wasn't afraid of hard work and labored feverishly when necessary to keep the shop going. His father had never missed an opportunity to scold him about keeping up the business or the importance of earning one's pay. It was a useful tactic for getting young Edwin Jr. to work for free, and it became the only education or religion Edwin Sr. would instill. These values followed Edwin into adulthood, and they had helped him overcome tough times. Yet, he had never much taken to societal norms and decorum—another reason Mr. Wilkinson did not approve of his relationship with Lillian. He viewed her affection for Edwin as a complete affront to the traditional Boston Brahmin upbringing he aimed to instill, which it was.

Mr. Wilkinson was a shrewd man, a staunchly conservative Catholic who managed a commercial fleet operating out of Boston Harbor. He could be seen around the port whenever a company vessel was being readied for departure, berating crew or arguing taxes and code violation fees with harbor officials. His diligence had paid off. Over a span of twenty-some years, he'd built a small fishing business into one of the eastern seaboard's busiest and most efficient trade fleets. Mr. Wilkinson had amassed great wealth, and the family lived lavishly because of it. Ironically, it was thanks to Mr. Wilkinson that Edwin and Lillian met—a fact Mr. Wilkinson never wanted to be reminded of.

* * *

It was a humid day in spring when Mr. Wilkinson's chauffeur-driven carriage bearing his proud company name parked directly in front of Edwin's shop. Two groomed horses stomped their feet and nagged as Mr. Wilkinson, a portly, well-put-together older man, stepped down holding black leather spats in his gold-ringed fingers. Edwin was inside laboring over a pair of clogs, peering through the shop window as Mr. Wilkinson marched toward the front door. Edwin thought the worst, sure he was about to be informed of another debt. He stiffened his posture and acted even busier than he was as Mr. Wilkinson, troubled by the wracked door's rusty hinges, entered the shop, looking down his nose at the messy workspace and the young cobbler sitting within it. Mr. Wilkinson wore pressed trousers, a thick felt duster, and a pair of Oxfords. A dagger-sharp contrast to Edwin's cotton shirt and dirty leather apron. "I should hope you repair boots better than you fix doors," Mr. Wilkinson barked.

"I'm a cobbler, not a carpenter," Edwin quipped right back. They disliked each other from the start. Mr. Wilkinson judged Edwin for his filthy appearance and seeming complacency regarding the upkeep of his business. Edwin returned prejudice, disgusted by Mr. Wilkinson's arrogant posture, piggish nose, and sneering expression.

"The flaps on these spats are getting loose and the left pad has come undone," Mr. Wilkinson said, holding them up for Edwin to see.

"You work at the harbor, I take it?" Edwin asked, inspecting the boots.

"I own the harbor," Mr. Wilkinson replied righteously.

"Saltwater breaks the leather down quicker. You want me to repair them?"

Mr. Wilkinson crossed his arms. "If the price is right."

"I'm sure my fee wouldn't be missed from your holdings," Edwin said, appealing to Mr. Wilkinson's sense of stature in hopes he wouldn't haggle over the cost.

"I'm sure it wouldn't," Mr. Wilkinson fired back.

Edwin hid a smirk, believing the price was now his to name. Of the handful of tactics that stuck from his upbringing, the art of negotiating had proven the most useful. Ed relished a good back-and-forth. "Three dollars. Buck fifty per boot," he said assuredly, as if it were the set price for such a repair. Three dollars was nothing to Mr. Wilkinson, but to Edwin it was a week's worth of tobacco and hoppins and a barrel of firewood from Porter's market cart.

"Two dollars. One dollar per boot," Mr. Wilkinson fired back, equally prone to haggling.

Edwin thought on it for a moment, visibly calculating the cost of labor, materials, and the added snob tax aptly due. He scanned the shop bench, trying to muster up the courage to make a counter. *Two fifty or go fuck yourself,* Edwin wanted to say. Instead, he said, "Two dollars it is."

"Good," Mr. Wilkinson replied, un-amused. "How long?"

"A few days," Edwin said with recourse, knowing he could do it in an afternoon.

Ever the shrewdest businessman in the room, Mr. Wilkinson saw right through him. "You'll have them done tomorrow, and deliver them to me at my office," he snarled. Edwin nodded subordinately as Mr. Wilkinson scooted loose material off the workbench, placing his boots in the space with distinction.

"Your name, sir? For the work order," Edwin inquired.

"Herman P. Wilkinson. Wilkinson Shipping Lines. State Street and Central Wharf."

Edwin nodded, pretending like he hadn't heard of him before, not wanting to give Mr. Wilkinson the satisfaction. "Spats'll be good as new by tomorrow afternoon," he said.

"They better be," Mr. Wilkinson muttered, turning to leave without tipping his hat.

Edwin hated him, and considered sewing rocks and uneven replacement pads inside each boot so that Mr. Wilkinson's feet would be sore whenever he wore them, and that over time he might develop a crooked back and a limping step. On the other hand, Edwin figured a job well done could get his own sore feet in the doors of high-society customers needing repair work. He imagined there were plenty of busted boots hoarded in the closets of South Boston's elite. Of course, in addition to being more tightfisted than most of his contemporaries—many of whom would simply have sprung for new boots—Mr. Wilkinson was not the type to provide a reference for the likes of Edwin, nor admit to employing a port cobbler in the first place.

Still, Edwin gave Mr. Wilkinson's boots due diligence, finishing the job on schedule with precision and pride, as he would any of his other repairs. It may not have been apparent to Mr. Wilkinson on the day they met, but Edwin was a craftsman at heart. Although he'd rather have spent the day drinking and drawing, Edwin was a man of his word and always completed a job. The boots were to be as good as new, and the next day, Edwin polished them up before making his way to port for delivery.

The midday sun bounced off the ocean and spread across the wet docks and glass-fronted shanties that populated the port blocks. Chimneys exhaled smoke into the wind, permeating the air. This part of town was always a study in dissimilitude to Edwin. Clean men of industry on their way to work rushed past wretched men of sorrow on their way to or from the saloon. Fresh-suited entrepreneurs and fish-covered crewmen occupied the same market cafes that had lined that part of town for decades. Harbor business aside, most decent folks didn't come around unless they were chasing vice. It pleased Edwin to know that, for once, he was here on business. He passed barrels and stacked shipping containers along Broad Street on his way toward the central wharf, to a large looming office building near the slips. Hung-over seaman loaded a deep draft vessel for its long journey as Edwin reached the arched entrance of the Wilkinson Shipping Lines headquarters. He tapped his boots clean before stepping inside.

Edwin made his way through the bustling office, admiring the world maps, depth charts, and work orders lining the walls. Nearby, a group of men pried open drums and sacks full of molasses, taking inventory. Edwin politely asked them where he could find Mr. Wilkinson. A tall gent holding a clipboard and wearing a top hat pointed crudely to a set of stairs, too busy to utter a word or make eye contact. Edwin nodded and continued on, scaling the stairs and coming to a stop just outside a grand office. Mr. Wilkinson sat behind a large oak desk piled with binders and paperwork. Tall windows surrounded the office, affording him a nearly 360-degree view of the happenings out on the floor. Edwin knocked twice on the doorframe, and though Mr. Wilkinson barely glanced up from the manifest he was studying, he managed to snarl as Edwin approached. "Spats and pads all fixed up, then?" he said in an oddly accusatory tone.

"Better than new," Edwin replied proudly. "I reinforced the soles as well, and gave them a nice polish." Edwin cleared a space on the crowded desk to place them on display for approval.

"Take those boots off my desk!" Mr. Wilkinson demanded, without even looking at them. Edwin bit his tongue and obliged, placing them on the floor beside the desk instead. "I'm not paying for any of that extra work, either."

"Of course," Edwin said, while thinking, *Fuck you.* "I did that as a courtesy."

"Good," Mr. Wilkinson replied. "That will be all."

"And my fee, sir?" Edwin asked.

"My accountant won't be in for another hour. Go wait in the lobby. He'll pay you the dollar owed."

"It's two dollars, sir. A dollar per boot."

Mr. Wilkinson looked up for the first time, eyeballing Edwin disdainfully before waving him off. Edwin grit his teeth, turning to leave and making his way to a bench in the lobby. He waited for nearly two hours before Wilkinson's accountant showed up. The accountant wore a smart-looking wool suit and was drunk from the night before. Edwin stopped him in the lobby and informed him of the payment.

"Ah, yes, the cobbler from Summer Street…the amount due again was what?"

"Three dollars," Edwin replied slyly. The accountant may have questioned the amount, but not enough to withhold payment.

"Very well," he said, opening his folio to retrieve three bills and handing them to Edwin with a fake smile. Edwin took the money and gave the accountant a sarcastic tip of his hat. When the accountant scuttled off, Edwin grinned to himself, walking toward the door in a hurry.

And there she was…Lillian…hopping down from a private carriage, bearing effortless radiance that struck Edwin instantly. Their eyes locked and she seemed equally caught by him, sizing up his boyish good looks and broad shoulders. The smirk he'd left the accountant with twisted into a shy grin as he held the door open for her. *You are beyond a sight for sore eyes*, Edwin wanted to say un-foolishly, instead blurting out, "You make my eyes hurt."

"Is that a good thing?" she asked, smiling. He was nervous, and she found it adorable.

Edwin beamed. "I meant to say, you are absolutely beautiful. It caught me off guard."

Lillian blushed and lightly tugged on her hair. "I haven't seen you around here before. Are you doing work for my father?"

"Your father?" Edwin asked, straightening his coat and posture.

"Yes. I'm Lillian Wilkinson, pleased to meet you."

"Lillian," Edwin repeated, committing her name to his heart. "My name is Edwin Morris. I repaired a pair of spats for your father. I own a shop not far from here." He felt dignified for the first time in a long while.

"A fine job it was then, I'm sure, otherwise my father would not have paid you," Lillian replied, noting the cash in his hand. "Perhaps you should pocket those bills, though. The riff-raff around here may take you for a mark."

"You're probably right," Edwin said, "although I don't think anyone will be looking at my hands when they have you to gaze upon." He smiled as he pocketed the money, never taking his eyes from her. He was overcome by her confidence and beauty.

Lillian smiled and looked away, feeling suddenly shy. They stood together in the doorway, seemingly frozen in time, until the chauffeur, a mean-looking wolf of a man in fine threads, piped up from the carriage, "This fink bothering you, Ms. Wilkinson?"

"Not yet, Strickland," Lillian replied, waving the chauffer off to mind his business.

"Your father is waiting for you," Strickland said smugly.

"He'll wait a little while longer, then, and so will you," she said, clearly in command of the situation. Strickland turned away, not daring to argue. Edwin gulped and straightened his vest. Lillian was intrigued. Edwin was in love.

"Do you have plans for lunch?" he asked with all the confidence he could muster.

"Perhaps I do now," she said, placing a hand delicately on his arm. "I'll just be a moment, if you don't mind waiting."

"I'll wait for as long as it takes," Edwin said with a slight tip of his hat. Lillian smiled and curtsied in return before heading inside. Strickland glared from the carriage, but Edwin paid him no mind as he walked over to a nearby viewpoint of the harbor to wait patiently with a wide smile plastered across his face. Lillian returned as promised, instructing Strickland to leave them alone while they strolled along the pier.

* * *

The percolator finished brewing. Edwin poured coffee into a ceramic mug and stirred in a spoonful of sugar before taking an addict's gulp. It was harsh, chalky, and strong, just how he liked it. He yanked a work apron off its hook and searched the room for a pencil and buck slip, finding them under a newssheet before heading downstairs. He couldn't wait to be done with this place, and vowed to never look back once he started working for Mr. Wilkinson.

Daylight was just starting to peek through the windows as Edwin took his place at the cluttered bench in the middle of the room. He spent the next several hours working tirelessly to complete the due order, frequently checking a small grandfather clock in the corner to track his progress. It was afternoon when a horse-drawn cart full of market goods pulled up on the street outside the shop. Edwin went to greet the man driving it. Porter was his name, a slightly hunched fellow with a long beard and straw hat. He and Edwin had become something close to friends over the years. Porter owned a modest supply store and would also make rounds through the boroughs with goods stuffed into his cart for sale or barter. "Good morning, Mr. Morris. How be you today?" Porter said as he hopped down from the driving seat.

"I won't complain," Edwin said as they shook hands. "Unless you're out of twists?"

"I've four or five in tow, I think, with more back at the shop if need be."

"I'll take what twists you have on the cart. Could use a few bundles of wood too."

Porter nodded proudly as he dug through the stow, picking out tobacco twists and handing them over before unloading a few bundles of wood from a side hitch. Edwin pocketed the tobacco as he and Porter carried the bundles to a dry storage trunk on the side of the building. "How's business?" Porter asked casually.

"Comes and goes. Will be closing for good soon, when Lillian's father comes through with the new position he's promised," Edwin replied.

"Well, I'd hope you refer me as a vendor once you have any say with them high-society folk," Porter said with a suggestive grin.

"You may not want me as a reference," Edwin said as they heaved the wood into place. "Her father has never cared much for me."

"No man cares much for the man plugging his daughter. You'll see one day when you have children," Porter said as they walked back to the parked cart.

Edwin shrugged. He couldn't argue. "I suppose so. And how is your family, then?"

"The wife's getting plump and the kids are getting old, so life is better than I deserve," Porter said. Edwin laughed, and Porter secured the cargo rope on his cart.

"What do I owe ya?" Edwin asked.

"Call us even at seventy-five cents," Porter replied, stepping back up into his seat. Edwin counted out the coins and handed them over, then went back inside to finish the last of the day's work.

When he had completed the order, Edwin packed boots into a crate and lugged it out for delivery. It was well into the afternoon when he finally returned home from the port with an empty crate and five dollars in earnings. He scurried up to the loft and dug out his best trousers and coat to wear for the anniversary party, then donned the black low-top hat he stored wrapped in newssheets to keep clean for such special occasions. He only had a few decent threads, and it was getting harder to keep them in rotation without eliciting judgment from the Wilkinsons and their peers. Not that Lillian cared—everything about Edwin appealed to her, even his shabby wardrobe—but Edwin still wished to make a good impression, or at least be given credit for his efforts. He even waxed his mustache before heading off, something his father would have certainly considered a foolish waste of time.

He began his trip by crossing Washington Street to a small market that sold flower arrangements, picking out the most colorful bouquet he could afford before continuing south. Ramshackle wooden buildings like his own gave way to the regal neighborhoods across the South Boston bridge. The Wilkinson estate sat on a wide and bright corner lot, replete with gardens and trees. Edwin waited for carriages to clear before crossing the paved street leading to the front gate of their manicured homestead. It generally took only an hour for him to walk there, but he may as well have traveled to another continent for how out of sorts the place made him feel. He wiped sweat away from his brow and took a deep breath as he marched forward. Strickland stood guard near the entrance per usual, smoking a cigarette. Edwin nodded politely and tried to move past, but Strickland held his hand up.

"Not tonight, rum-dum," Strickland said.

"This charade is tired. You know damn well I was invited."

"Well now you're damn well uninvited," Strickland sneered. "Boss says no, so get."

"Where is Lillian?"

"She's inside—where you ain't."

"You're out of line, and a half-wit pain in the ass."

"Watch it, beefer..." Strickland warned, pulling his duster back to reveal a holstered revolver on his hip.

Edwin held his ground. "I demand to speak with Lillian."

Just then, Mr. Wilkinson emerged from the front door several yards away. Music and laughter escaped from within the lavish house behind him until the door shut. "Get on, Morris," he said, marching closer. "I've made up my mind, and this time it's going to stick."

"Mr. Wilkinson, goddamn it, we've been through this," Edwin pleaded.

"Indeed, we have," Mr. Wilkinson spat. "But this time, I'm not letting anyone squawk and change my mind about it. I'll be damned if I have some low-class cobbling runt in my home unless he's here to fix the shitter. And even then, it won't be you! My foot is down firm."

Edwin protested further, reminding the old man that Lillian and he were to be married.

"Over my cold, dying body!" Mr. Wilkinson snarled. "Scram while you can."

"I'm not going anywhere until I see Lillian."

"You will," Strickland said, pulling the revolver and cocking its hammer back. Edwin grit his teeth and took a hesitant step back.

"Let this be the last time I see you," said Mr. Wilkinson.

"You're a coward and a liar," Edwin said. "Does your word mean nothing?"

"It means less to me than the security of my only daughter, which you are not fit to uphold," Mr. Wilkinson said calmly. "Now go quiet on your own, before I have Strickland here drag you away in a sack."

"This isn't over," Edwin fumed, tossing the flowers down as he turned to leave. Strickland watched him storm off, and Mr. Wilkinson, satisfied, went back inside.

Edwin stewed and rumbled with rage as he passed through lantern-lit neighborhoods that degraded as he plodded north, finally making it back to the edge of the harbor district and into a saloon he knew well. Before meeting Lillian, Edwin frequented pubs. He loved their familiar commotion, but mostly he loved getting drunk. He'd spend a day's earnings getting sloshed on thick bourbon, just to fight the headache throughout the next day and do it all over again. Boredom and regrets—he washed them down this way night after night. Lillian had inspired him to change his ways, and now he drank tea most nights instead, trying to prove to himself, and Mr. Wilkinson, that he was worthy of her love. That he was the better man Mr. Wilkinson always accused him of not being— or at least, perhaps, he could be. Still, he and Lillian occasionally went to a pub together to escape the world she felt trapped in, a world that Edwin didn't belong in to begin with. He knew that if Lillian wanted to see him, she would know to look for him here at this particular pub, set nearly halfway between the divide of geography keeping them apart.

Edwin sat at the bar and ordered hot tea, but several hours passed in the smoky saloon full of hobos and seamen and Lillian never showed up. Even if he wanted to keep waiting, Edwin couldn't afford even another round of air. He settled his tab and begrudgingly went on his way. *It can't just end like this*, he thought. *Not without a fight.* A renewed conviction marched him back to the Wilkinsons' home. If Lillian wanted him gone, so be it, but if this were merely another ruse by Mr. Wilkinson, then Edwin was willing to fight it out. Strickland and his revolver be damned.

It was too early to be morning and too late to be night by the time Edwin made it back to the Wilkinson estate. Lillian's second-story window was dark. There was no sign of her or anyone else as he crept along the gate, peeking through hedges, trying to get a glimpse of Lillian or find a way in besides the front gate. "Not so fast, rum-dum," Strickland said, looming around the corner with his revolver aimed. "Mr. Wilkinson thought you might try coming back, but to be honest, I didn't think you had the sand."

"I don't care what you or your owner says, pet," Edwin fumed, stepping closer. "Until I hear from Lillian that she wants me gone, I'm going nowhere, and you can't do fuck-all about it!"

"Is that a fact, you scrawny cunt?"

"As much a fact as your zook mother regrets having you," Edwin said, caught up in the moment. Strickland snarled, then smiled widely.

"Good…Now I get to tamp you up…" Strickland raised his revolver, then twisted his grip and racked Edwin in the head with its handle. Edwin went down hard, grabbing at his temple. Strickland followed up with a couple of swift kicks to the gut, enjoying every moment. "If you want, I can finish ya off now too?" he said, backing up to aim the revolver at Edwin's head. Edwin stayed down and held his gut, groaning and spitting blood.

"Strickland!" Mr. Wilkinson hollered as he approached, hawk-like, from the front gate. Another guard aiming a rifle and holding up a lantern accompanied him. "Stand down!"

Edwin perked up, relieved that Mr. Wilkinson had come to his aid, until Wilkinson himself began screaming at Edwin. "Where is she? Where's my daughter, you son of a bitch?" Mr. Wilkinson launched a kick into Edwin's gut.

"I came here looking for her!" Edwin pleaded through coughing gasps.

"She left hours ago in a fit!" Mr. Wilkinson raged, kicking Edwin again. "You're going to tell me you haven't been with her and expect me to believe that?"

"Why the fuck would I be here if I was already with her?" Edwin screamed. Which actually made sense to Mr. Wilkinson, and so he took a beat to catch his breath.

Just then, a horse-drawn cart pulled up with two farmers scrambling off. "Mr. Wilkinson?" one of them asked, his voice trembling.

"I am," Mr. Wilkinson said, turning to face the men as they descended their buggy.

"I'm afraid we have your daughter here, sir. She was in a terrible accident."

Mr. Wilkinson's eyes went wild. Edwin hopped to his feet. They ran to the back of the cart and pulled a blanket away, revealing Lillian awash in blood. Her face was bruised, and her body was limp. They explained that she had been trampled by

27

a runaway carriage while crossing a street across the bridge. Edwin was momentarily calmed in the certainty that she'd been out looking for him. The farmers had witnessed the accident, and when they went to Lillian's aid, they recognized the family crest on her purse. They carted her back to the Wilkinson home as fast as they could, but it was too late. She had succumbed to the wounds. Lillian was dead.

2

PASSING TIME

Treslyn lands and Tre...
Heir nor heiress e...
Undisturbed, still...
Truth is found ...

"This ... th... I've found you poring over the old rhyme. What is the ..., Richard? Not its poetry I fancy," ... young wife ..., she ... her hand on ... low, tim... ... where, ... old Engl... text, ap... ... lines sh...

Rich... Tre... looked up ... mile a... ... book, a... f... ... at being discovered reading ... Drawi... ... wife's h... in his own, he led her back to her couch, ... the soft ... about her, and, sitting in a low chair besi... ... said in a cheer... ... hough his eyes betrayed ... hidde... ... "My love, tha... ... story of our family for c...turies, ... at old prophecy ... n... ... been fulfilled, ... heiress" line. I am the last ... lyn, and as the time ... when my child shall be born ... naturally think of his future, ... I hope he will enjoy his heritage ...

"God grant ..." ... Lad... Tre... odding, with a look as... ... th... ... ... once, and fancied it must ... ... orded in it. Is it all tru... ... ... ld, unhappy ... ... me in with ... ... u i...

The funeral several days later was a formal event attended by everyone who was anyone in South Boston. Marie Wilkinson sobbed as Lillian's glossy oak casket was lowered into its final resting place. Herman Wilkinson consoled her, attempting to remain stoic. Edwin looked on from a distance, holding flowers and dressed for mourning. The boozing and despair had aged him a year in less than a week. He was overdue for a bath and a shave, but for the most part had managed to put himself together, straining tired and baggy eyes to see the proceedings from afar. He wasn't invited to the funeral, which meant he was not allowed to go per Mr. Wilkinson's harsh rulings in the aftermath of Lillian's death. He had never been kind to Edwin but had since become filled with an utter loathing of him. For the tragedy of Lillian's passing, Edwin was blamed and banished.

Strickland loomed halfway between Edwin and the mourners, keeping an eye on both and a hand on his holstered revolver, sneering and spitting tobacco. Edwin snarled back and debated picking a fight just so he could feel something other than grief. Maybe even death was better than how he felt.

So much rage. So much loss. He was consumed by it. He wondered if Lillian's death really was his fault. She wouldn't have been crossing that broken street in the first place if she hadn't gone to look for him at the pub. He had not been able to stop himself from reeling over the events of that night, wishing he could take it all back and choking on his sadness. He was a wreck of self-destruction, drowning himself in alcohol and boiling over with anger every time he got cut off by the proprietor of whatever saloon he left fall-down drunk from each night. He'd sleep in piss in the alleys. He had gotten no work done at the shop and refused to take on any new orders.

The minister gave a thoughtful eulogy before friends and family took turns sharing stories about Lillian—not that Edwin could hear any of them. After the ceremony, mourners wished the family well and began returning to their carriages or walking home. Edwin rolled a cigarette as the crowd spread out. Some passed by with looks of disdain, while others gave compassionate nods of condolence. Edwin gave them all the same stone-faced grimace in return. He lit his cigarette and took deep drags between gulps from a bottle of whiskey fetched from his coat pocket. He stiffened his posture as Mr. and Mrs. Wilkinson began to head his way, toward their carriage parked just behind him.

Mr. Wilkinson was interrupted by one of his business associates and hung back to discuss what appeared to be a time-sensitive subject, considering the location of the meeting. Mrs. Wilkinson continued on, leaving them to talk and heading right for Edwin. Edwin tried hiding in plain sight, turning his back to inhale his cigarette as she approached. "Edwin?" Marie said with an inflection somewhere between blame and remorse. Edwin slowly turned to face her, and was reminded instantly of Lillian's eyes and fair skin. Mrs. Wilkinson handed him a small box wrapped in a colorful fabric. "Lillian wanted you to have this," she said solemnly. "It was to be a gift for your…well, she wanted you to have it."

Edwin didn't know what to say. A posthumous wedding gift was the furthest thing from his mind. He took it with a shaky hand but couldn't bring himself to speak. Mrs. Wilkinson looked through Edwin like he wasn't even there. Her eyes were swollen and full of tears, which she quickly wiped away. Mr. Wilkinson noticed the exchange and shifted to intercept. "It's time to go, Marie," he said with a soft intensity as he marched over to them.

"Take care of yourself," she whispered to Edwin, brushing her hand across his shoulder before walking away toward the family carriage. Edwin pocketed the gift and tossed his cigarette as Mr. Wilkinson approached with Strickland on his heels. Edwin raised his chin, making himself taller and mentally preparing for a fight.

"My only wish is to live long enough to piss on your grave," Mr. Wilkinson said, face to face, trembling with rage and practically daring Edwin to step out of line. Instead, Edwin stood his ground and returned the glare ten-fold, leaving nothing for Mr. Wilkinson to do but spit at his feet and move on.

"Give me a reason..." Strickland said while brandishing his holster and obediently following Mr. Wilkinson. But Edwin didn't take Strickland's bait either. Instead, he tipped his whiskey bottle toward Strickland, sarcastically offering him a pull. Strickland almost took it, too, letting his guard down for a brief moment before Edwin spitefully rescinded and took a hearty gulp from the bottle himself. Strickland huffed and kicked rocks, following his master.

Edwin watched them all leave together in the family carriage before pocketing the whiskey and slowly making his way over to Lillian's gravesite. Her headstone was made of marble and tastefully done. Edwin stood there alone and motionless, choking back tears. "I'll never forget you, my love. The times we shared were the best moments of my life," he whispered sweetly, kneeling down to take a fistful of the fresh dirt covering her grave. He looked around, as if seeking from the air some sort of answer or meaning. He reached into his pocket for Lillian's gift, afraid to open it but finally removing the soft blue cloth to reveal a brand-new silver and mahogany harmonica. He burst into tears and clutched the instrument against his heart.

* * *

It was a bright summer evening with calm, cooling winds. Edwin had just finished the day's workload and was tidying up the small storage room at the back of his shop. A light knock on the front door snapped him out of it. It was Lillian. She had been at the harbor and decided to surprise Edwin with a visit. He opened the busted shop door and was elated to see her standing there, lovely in a plaid silk taffeta dress with that smile he'd die for. "Well, good evening," Edwin said. "I wasn't expecting to see you until day after tomorrow. A pleasant surprise you are."

"I do hope it's all right to call unannounced," Lillian replied.

"Absolutely, sweetheart. Always," Edwin said, inviting her in and then wrestling to close the door. He glanced out the window, looking for Strickland or other staff, but there was none. Either she had been dropped off or she'd walked there, which Edwin excitedly took as a sign that Lillian planned on staying for a while, perhaps even overnight. They had been dating for nearly two months and their electricity was magnetic and intense. They had frequented local cafes and gone on long walks around town, but this was the first time Lillian had visited Edwin in the evening. She'd been to the shop before, but had never been upstairs to the loft. Lillian loved that Edwin worked with his hands and was interested in fixing and tinkering with things. Edwin loved that she loved that about him. Lillian was so learned and well-traveled, and yet was never cavalier about it. Her stories of visiting Europe and Asia as a child inspired Edwin to see past the shores of Boston harbor. He hoped to travel now, and looked forward to all of the adventures they would embark on together someday. They each admired traits in the other they had wished they possessed in themselves. They were happy and in love.

Edwin cleared a spot for her to sit on the workbench and clasped his hands in a serviceable fashion. "Would you like a tea or coffee? Have you eaten?"

"Some tea would be wonderful," Lillian said with a smile.

"Tea it is. I'll only be a moment," he replied, pivoting to head upstairs.

"May I see your loft?" she asked with that smile. Edwin paused, slightly shrugging.

"There's not much to see," he said, knowing it was a mess upstairs. "But, of course, you can come up."

Edwin was thrilled and nervous as Lillian entered the loft with him. He quickly made his bed and adjusted some clutter on the desk, hoping she wouldn't think less of him for the squalor. Apparently, she did not, and stood fascinated by the collection of drawings hung along the wall. "Are these yours?" she asked.

"They are," Edwin replied somewhat shyly, while building a fire in the oven's base.

"They're really wonderful," she said. Edwin didn't know how to respond. No one had ever seen his drawings before, let alone told him they were any good.

"Mostly a hobby. Helps pass the time."

"Are all of your renderings done on newssheets?" she asked playfully.

Edwin laughed. "Why waste a canvas?"

"Well, I think they're great."

Edwin smiled and looked away, nervous. Having a beautiful woman in his living area was uncharted territory. He stayed busy filling a kettle and heating it on the stove while Lillian looked around some more, noting his clothes and knick-knacks and taking it all in. She scanned the desk and found a beat-up and rusty harmonica. "Do you play?" she asked, holding it up.

Edwin nodded remorsefully. "I used to."

"Why not anymore?"

"It's a bit of a story," he admitted. She smiled, eager to hear it and get to know him better. Edwin poured the tea into mismatched mugs, handing the less chipped one to Lillian. He went on to tell her that his favorite uncle, his father's brother Walton, had given him the harmonica as a young boy and always encouraged him to practice. Edwin got good and he played it all the time. He was eleven when Uncle Walton was killed fighting for the Union as part of the 6th Massachusetts militia. His unit was attacked in Baltimore on their way to Washington D.C. by a pro-secession mob. It crushed Edwin Sr. even more than it did Edwin Jr., which was saying a lot. Playing the harmonica became taboo after Walton's death; its music troubled Edwin Sr. more and more, until he banned his son from playing it altogether. Drawing became Edwin's silent replacement and creative outlet. He used charcoal and graphite because they were free or cheap and abundant around town.

"Your uncle—what a sad story," Lillian said while sipping her tea. "Maybe you'll pick up playing music again someday."

"That rusty old thing?" Edwin laughed, shaking his head.

"You never know," she replied, after a moment of reflection.

"What I do know is that you are the most radiant creature I've ever seen," he said, all love-struck and starry-eyed. "I wish I could spend all of my time with you."

Lillian blushed and bit her upper lip. Her smile turned from charming to suggestive as she placed her teacup down and motioned for Edwin to come closer. "You are a handsome craftsman and artist, and the best-kept secret in this rotten old town," she said tenderly, pulling him into an embrace.

"I love you, Lillian," he said softly.

"I love you too, Edwin."

They grasped on to each other, kissing deeply and easing their play onto the cot. It was the first time either of them had made love, and the best night of Edwin's life.

* * *

Edwin stood solemnly over Lillian's grave, letting dirt fall from his hand. "I'll miss you forever," he said with a tremble in his voice, carefully wrapping the harmonica back up into its cloth and placing it in his coat pocket. He took another swig of whiskey, then pulled his collar tight as the moaning wind warned of a coming storm. It wasn't easy, but Edwin turned his back to Lillian's final resting place and walked away. He vowed never to return.

Edwin lurched along Broad Street, drunk and mumbling to himself. Lillian's death had dismembered his emotional well-being. He'd been prepared to devote his life to her and couldn't conceive of anything else worth living for now that she was gone. He could no longer even tolerate being surrounded by the neighborhoods where he had grown up and fallen in love. Everything he saw had a memory attached to it. The memories he wanted to keep were even harder to bear than the memories he wished he could forget. He needed an escape but had nowhere to go and no funds. Edwin's thoughts swirled with wanderlust as he charged on. He was exhausted. The gloomy haze he'd been wallowing in had nearly broken him completely, but now it was time to snap out of it or just kill himself and be done with it already. Something, if not everything, needed to change.

It was getting dark, and the wind continued to howl as Edwin reached Summer Street. He was sick of staring at the busted shop baring his worthless name. The whiskey bottle in his pocket was empty, and he knew there wasn't any wood stored to keep the loft warm. It seemed like all this tumbledown town had to offer Edwin was despair. He waved off and continued toward Bedferd Street to stop in at a tavern he knew well. The rustic joint was drenched in shadows and full of smoke. It smelled like old beer and body odor—the calling card of taverns near the harbor catering to dock workers and sailors.

Monty, the crusty and aged tavern owner, recognized Edwin from a particularly reckless bender a few nights before and raised his hand in protest. "No way," Monty said. "Gots any money or ya merely here to mooch? Made me regret feeling sorry fer ya."

"I have two shiners," Edwin said, holding up a pair of ten-cent coins.

"That's not even half of makin' ya even for last time. Give 'em here," Monty demanded.

Edwin hesitated but handed the coins over with a scowl. "Can I have a drink?"

"Not on credit. You still owe."

"That was the last of my coin," Edwin contended. "Just one drink? I'll be by tomorrow to square us up."

"Then tomorrow ya can drink. Until then, ya can kick cobble," Monty said, turning his back and moving over to tend to another patron who could actually pay.

Fucking hell, Edwin thought. "I'll be by tomorrow," he said to Monty's back. He was broke and sobering up—a terrible combination for his newly adopted vagabond lifestyle. He decided to wander home, bundle himself up in bed, and reevaluate things with fresh eyes in the morning.

The new day came far quicker than Edwin had hoped it would as he slid out of bed to get a pot of coffee going. Not only was he hung over, he now had to face the promises he'd made to himself the night before about putting his affairs in order and getting out of Boston. All easier said drunk at night than done sober in the light of day. Just then, Porter pulled up in his market cart outside, sparking an idea. He threw his trousers and frock coat on and hurried downstairs, nearly tripping on the last step and barely avoiding a collision with the cabinet. Edwin kicked the shop door open and marched up to the curb. "Porter! Good morning!"

"Afternoon, ain't it?" Porter replied, chuckling. "Jesus, Edwin, you look like vampire shit," he added upon taking a closer look.

"Never mind that. I have a proposition for you," Edwin said.

"I'm listening…" Porter said, stuffing a wad of tobacco into his mouth.

"I'm making tracks, for good. Wondering if you might be interested in any of the tools and fixtures from my shop?"

Porter rubbed his chin. "Leaving town, ay?"

"Indeed. Starting over anew, selling everything I own to fund travel," Edwin said, as if he'd conceived this plan prior to just now as he spoke.

"Well, shit—yeah, I'm interested." Porter hawked a stream of chew spit.

"Excellent," Edwin said contentedly. "Come in and let's take a look."

Edwin led Porter inside. Over the next hour, they negotiated the exchange of all of Edwin's tools, two cabinets, and an assortment of leather and felt for fifty dollars, six twists of tobacco, and a wholesaler's tin of pre-ground coffee. It was a good deal for both of them, right down the middle. Edwin even helped secure the cabinets onto Porter's cart and threw in the rope to do so for free. They shook hands and Porter hopped up into his seat. "Be well, Mr. Morris," Porter said, grabbing the reigns. "I wish ya all the luck in the world."

"You as well. Been a pleasure," Edwin said, patting Porter's horse on the hind leg to help get him and the cart going. Edwin watched Porter drive off, weighing the sack of goods and money in his hand. He couldn't remember the last time he'd held fifty dollars, and it felt plum—but now what? The only other asset he had was the deed to his father's shop. He had considered selling in the past but was always afraid of what he'd do for work without it. That didn't matter anymore. Edwin stomped upstairs to dig out his best trousers and vest, throwing them on in a hurry before waxing his hair back and kicking on a pair of togs. He searched through the desk's cabinet for the land deed, finding it at the bottom of a stack of completed work orders left over from when his father was alive and actually kept prudent records. Edwin scanned the deed remorsefully, pondering how hard it must have been for his parents to save up for the shop, and how happy and excited they were upon doing so. *Only to end up widowed and alone, dying in debt, leaving it all to an un-earning half-pint spawn who'd later hawk the place to get out of town*, Edwin thought. He knew now more than ever how crushing the weight of losing a spouse was, and he felt sorry for his senior for the first time in his life. It was a silent, fleeting revelation, but not by a long shot enough to stop him from selling the shop. And so, Edwin boldly headed for the harbor to seek council with the only man he knew with enough wealth to purchase land on the spot.

The port was bustling, as always. Waiting vessels buoyed in their slips as workers tended to loading and maintenance operations. Edwin approached the Wilkinson Shipping headquarters with some hesitation, collecting his thoughts outside the arched entrance before mustering on. Without whiskey, he'd have to rely on dry courage, a trait Edwin hadn't employed in some time. *Fuck you*, he thought, amping himself up as he entered. Mr. Wilkinson was sitting behind his desk scanning profit and loss ledgers when Edwin charged in, snarling. Mr. Wilkinson looked up, shocked and enraged to see Edwin looming over him.

"What the fucking hell are you doing here, Morris?" Mr. Wilkinson roared like a grizzly.

"I have a business proposition for you," Edwin said firmly.

"You and I have no business. Ever!" Mr. Wilkinson barked back. "I never wanted to see your sour mug again, now get!" Mr. Wilkinson dropped his ledgers and reached into his desk drawer for what Edwin presumed was a pistol.

"Hear me out," Edwin said, putting his hands up. "If you don't like my proposal, I'll leave without fuss. If not for me, then do it for..."

"Don't you dare say her name!" Mr. Wilkinson growled, standing fast with the pistol in his hand and aiming it right at Edwin's heart. Edwin didn't move or even blink. He just stood there, pleading with his eyes, allowing Mr. Wilkinson to pull the trigger and end his heartache for good. Mr. Wilkinson sensed this instantly too. He recognized Edwin's pain all too well. Finally, they had something in common. "Spit it out," Mr. Wilkinson said, chewing on his thoughts and humbly lowering the pistol.

"I'm skipping town for good. A few days, maybe a week," Edwin said as if he actually had a plan, pulling the deed from his coat and handing it over. "I'm selling my shop."

"What would I want with your broken-down cobbler box?" Mr. Wilkinson spat back, scanning the deed.

"The land it sits on, nearly a quarter acre in a rather undeveloped part of town," Edwin said, hoping Mr. Wilkinson could overlook his hatred in the name of greed. "Plus, I couldn't think of one other man of means more invested in getting me the hell over the road and out of sight forever," Edwin said to seal the deal. Mr. Wilkinson grumbled, pondering, and placed his pistol on the desk. He took a seat with his hands crossed inquisitively.

"How much?" Mr. Wilkinson asked, as if bothered by his own curiosity.

Edwin hadn't actually thought of a price but wanted his answer to appear as if he had. "Fifteen hundred paper notes, firm," he said sternly.

"Five hundred," Mr. Wilkinson replied.

"Twelve hundred," Edwin said with a tone indicating his disgust.

"No."

"Nine hundred," Edwin growled.

"Fine. When will you be leaving?"

"Notes up front and I'll be gone by end of the week."

"Notes up front and you'll be gone by midnight tomorrow."

"Fine," Edwin said, his mind racing. Nine hundred dollars meant that leaving town forever was now a possibility.

"So be it," Mr. Wilkinson said. Customarily, a handshake would have closed the deal, but neither of these men had any intention of shaking the other's hand without a knife fight. "I'll need to fetch my accountant to draw up the paperwork and pay you off," Mr. Wilkinson said, brushing past Edwin to emerge on the office balcony and yell for his accountant. Edwin nodded and feigned patience. He and Mr. Wilkinson stared away from each other in silence, both clenching their jaws and steaming awkwardly until the accountant finally scurried in. "Draw up a land buy for nine hundred dollars, with haste. We just bought a quarter acre on Summer Street.

The current mope needs to be out by midnight tomorrow or it's his ass!" Mr. Wilkinson barked, mostly for Edwin's benefit.

"Understood," the accountant said, then motioned to Edwin. "Follow me."

Edwin gave a reluctant nod to Mr. Wilkinson then left with the accountant.

"Morris," Mr. Wilkinson said, waiting for Edwin to turn back around. "This will be the last time we speak."

"On that, we also agree," Edwin said, sure they'd never cross paths again. Downstairs, the documents were executed, and Edwin was paid. *Good riddance, ya bastard*, he thought as he exited, then remembered how he'd first met Lillian in this very spot. Trudging toward Broad Street, he stuffed the money into his billfold, which now barely stayed shut. On a good week running the shop, before everything went to shit, Edwin could take home twenty dollars after expenses, so his now-bulging pocket represented unfamiliar territory and nearly a year's income. His next moves would be crucial.

"Well, look at this beefer," Strickland said, leaning against the wall of an alley adjacent to Wilkinson Shipping Lines. His hand rested casually on his holstered revolver. Edwin thought the man tried too hard to look menacing. He was sick of the ridicule. Feeling cocksure and impulsive, Edwin swung an elbow remorselessly into Strickland's face as he passed by, sending the guard reeling. Strickland grimaced and cupped his bloody nose, then quickly reached for his gun, but Edwin acted faster and yanked the revolver out of Strickland's holster. Edwin thumbed the hammer back and stuffed the barrel into Strickland's gut with a look that said, *You're mine now.* Strickland threw his hands up, gnashing his teeth and pleading with Edwin not to shoot.

Edwin had never shot a gun before, but he knew how they worked from the trades and wasn't afraid to shoot now. "You want the big sleep, lapdog?" he said callously. "I could just squeeze on ya and end this shit right now!" Edwin pushed the barrel harder into Strickland's gut. Strickland's nose was bleeding out onto his shirt, and his eyes were transparent with fear, bracing for the shot. Instead, Edwin turned the pistol around and slammed Strickland in his busted nose with the handle. Strickland's face cracked and oozed under the force. The blow launched him back into some crates stacked against the wall. "You fucking mouthpiece," Edwin muttered, looming over Strickland as he contorted in pain. He lifted his boot and launched a swift kick into the back of Strickland's head, knocking him out cold, then took a deep breath and scanned his surroundings. No one had seen the exchange. Edwin puffed his chest and calmly walked away, tossing Strickland's pistol into the water.

Edwin returned to his shop half an hour later, staring at it with new eyes, still swelling with pride from finally putting Strickland in line. Edwin had never been a violent man and didn't know what unexplored part of his soul the sand and swagger had come from, but he liked it. He felt a charge buzzing through his body and wanted to harness the feeling for future use. There wasn't much time to waste, and Edwin knew he would need to begin preparations for moving on. Instead, he kept walking until he reached the Bedferd Street Tavern, trading the setting orange sun behind him for the familiar darkness of the pub as he stepped inside. Monty shook his head from behind the bar, crossing his arms as Edwin approached. "You have a real thick head about this, don't ya?" Monty quipped.

"Today, just a thick wallet. I've come to square up and patronize," Edwin proclaimed, pulling out his stuffed billfold and fidgeting with his cash, a move that did not go unnoticed by two meatheads drinking in the corner nearby. "And now that we're even, I'll have some of your best whiskey on the double, and two pints of it to take with me." Edwin placed a five-dollar bill onto the bar. Monty nodded with surprise, took the five, and moved on to fetch the whiskey.

"You hit a streak of hobo luck or what?" Monty asked while pouring.

"I fucking hope so," Edwin said, gulping down the whiskey and encouraging Monty to pour another. "Don't forget my pints to go."

Monty returned with two pints, shaking his head as he placed them on the bar before tending to another patron. Edwin sipped whiskey and rolled a cigarette, going over everything he would have to do to get out of town the following day. Perhaps he could purchase a horse and buggy from the stable on Franklin Street and make his way north to New York City. Or pack light and get a ticket on the newly constructed steam engine locomotive heading west out of Worcester. Edwin had never had so many options at his disposal. He was unprepared to navigate them quickly, but his determination overpowered his lack of experience. He lit the cigarette and poured another drink, deciding the best idea was to head west as far as the railroad line would take him. He'd set up a new shop in an up-and-coming town or invest in an entirely fresh line of work—something established, perhaps an owner looking for partners. He was feeling more optimistic about his possibilities as he grabbed his pints, heading outside with a final wave goodbye. Monty did not wave back.

Edwin wasn't reassured by how dark and brumal it was as he exited the tavern, wondering how long he had been inside. The whiskey buzz had taken hold and he stumbled as he made his way. Then someone yelled behind him, "Palooka!" and

Edwin turned to meet a fist that smashed his face back and sent him hard to the ground. He dropped both whiskey bottles; one of them broke. The two meatheads from inside the pub stood over him, nearly indistinguishable in their sailor slickers and wool caps. The smaller, beefier one rubbed his fist and snarled, "You want a beating or ya just gonna hand that billfold over now?"

"Wait a minute..." Edwin slurred, trying to get to his feet.

BLAM—the shorter meathead launched his boot, kicking Edwin back down. The pummeling went on for a good minute and a half, leaving Edwin balled up on the ground and gripping his gut. The taller meathead had Edwin's wallet and whiskey, the shorter one had Lillian's harmonica. "We oughta hawk that," the taller one said.

"Nah. I kinda like it," the shorter meathead said, thumbing the harmonica.

The taller one shrugged contentedly, then pulled all of Edwin's cash out of the wallet and tossed the wallet to the ground. "Thanks much. Better luck next time," he said, kicking Edwin once more before they walked off.

Edwin spit blood and turned over on to his back, grimacing and slowly sobering up from the pain. A wash of sadness engulfed him as he realized they'd taken Lillian's harmonica. He had never even played it. All his money was gone, along with his whiskey, and in less than twenty-four hours, he would be homeless and unemployed. Edwin flattened out against the cold, wet cobblestone and stared up into the sky. The clouds moved in from the harbor and overtook the sea of stars above him. He laid there for what felt like hours, drowning in regret and confronting the terms of his situation. *What the fuck am I going to do now?*

3

FIRE AND WATER

"I must go in alone; fear nothing, but wait for me here," she said, and closed the door behind her.

Five minutes had not elapsed when she reappeared with no sign of ... and bring ... box," she said, with a ... faithful servant obeyed her with an

... had been obeyed ...
... which she always ...
... in a ...

MORRIS SHOEMAKING COMPANY

COBBLER

... whatever ... in comin ...
... reappeared ... covered. The cou ...
... Richard were not ... for the pau ...
... and no clue could be ...
... the physici ...

Edwin woke slowly in his loft, wearing the same damp-backed clothes from the night before. He hadn't even made it onto his cot, passing out on the floor as if a vagrant in his own home. Even though it wasn't his home anymore, at least not for long, as he had only until midnight to be cleared out per the terms with Mr. Wilkinson. Edwin was sober enough to know that he must abide. Mr. Wilkinson would certainly claim the money be returned if he didn't, and the money was gone. Plus, Edwin was sure it would be Strickland that came to collect before any lawmen, eager for a re-match and on the offensive about it. Edwin sought a blade to carry or maybe even a pistol, and not only for protection. He was furious over getting robbed and being unable to defend himself, and swore off letting it happen again.

Edwin collected his thoughts and belongings while fighting a hangover and waiting for the percolator to brew. He rolled a cigarette and took inventory of his holdings. He luckily still had the fifty dollars from bartering with Porter the day before left behind at the shop, but didn't have much else for supplies. Just some coffee and tobacco, along with chunks of charcoal and graphite, half a loaf of not-so-fresh bread, and small jars of sugar and beans. Edwin's new beginning seemed once again doomed as he inhaled his coffee and cigarette, straightening himself up without changing clothes. He plopped his hat on and exited the room. He had until midnight, but it was already midday. He didn't know where he was fixing to go or what he would do once he got there. Edwin didn't even bother wrestling with the shop's busted front door, leaving it ajar as he marched down Summer Street with troubles on his mind.

A steady rain poured over the commotion of activity on the port, but for Edwin, time was standing still. He passed busy storefronts full of folks buying goods and even busier dock slips full of hard-working men with more purpose than him. Edwin was out of place and on the bum, looking to get as far away from Boston as possible. For thirty dollars, damn near his entire purse, he could hop on a train and be in San Francisco within a week or two. Before drawing over the newssheet it was printed on, Edwin had once read about the great gold rush years back and thought there could be good employment opportunities for a young, unattached man to earn a living. Or perhaps New York was a more attainable option and he could find a steady craftsman to apprentice for. Edwin would be near depleted once again after the cost of such travel and yet was choking on possibility all at once.

Ahead of him was a well-dressed older businessman exiting a hat shop with a brand-new black-belled topper. Edwin only noticed because the businessman's billfold was protruding out of his coat pocket and he seemed completely aloof to it while focused on fitting the new hat using his reflection in the window. Edwin thought of how brazen he had been with his own billfold the night before, and that anyone who was as casual with their holdings as he had been might also deserve to be plundered. Edwin slowed to a stroll, peeking over his shoulders as he approached. Seeing that the coast was free of on-lookers, Edwin swiped the businessman's billfold as he passed. It was a clean steal. The man didn't notice and carried on in the other direction. Edwin ducked into an alley to take inventory of the score, feeling an adrenaline high for getting away with it—a welcome momentary relief to the anxious depression of getting jackrolled himself the night before. There was almost a hundred dollars in the man's billfold, a small fortune to Edwin now even more so than it would have been most other days. Edwin debated shoving the money into his own billfold or just adopting this new one. He went with the latter, ditching his own tired, empty wallet to the ground, then moving on with a sly demeanor.

The market Edwin arrived to was a small open-space building filled with a limited yet strategic inventory of food and supplies catered to harbor workers and poor scrubbers like himself. Everything was sold out of the drums and sacks it was shipped there in; sitting on the ground and arranged differently each time one would visit. Old Man Williams ran the place, and made a decent stew that he'd sell bowls of for cheap. Or just give a bowl out for free if a fella spent enough coin on supplies. Edwin perused the stock holding a wicker basket—collecting a jar of oats, six potatoes, two cornhusks, three apples, an onion, crackers, beef jerky, and two bottles of cheap potato vodka since there wasn't any whiskey for sale that day. All in all, it cost just under six dollars, and Old Man Williams even threw in a bowl of stew that Edwin chugged heartily. He left the market carrying a netted sack full of provisions, weaving between dockworkers as he plodded along the India Wharf. He ducked under a swinging ladder being carried by one of the workers just in time, avoiding a near head hit. *Well, maybe my shit luck is finally starting to change,* Edwin thought.

In the window of a fur trader's shop was a bone-handled knife stuffed into a leather sheath that caught Edwin's eye. He turned to head inside, knowing that he had to have it. The proprietor sat on a bearskin chair in the corner smoking a thick cigar. He was topped in a coyote pelt hat, looking every bit as used-up as the dry leather vest he was wearing crafted by his own two frowzy hands. The shop featured a row of wooden tables with raw pelts and furs on one side and completed blankets and clothing items piled high on the other. Nothing in this store would be cheap, but Edwin went right for the window display to examine the knife. "That's a fine piece," the fur trader said. "Forged steel with a chisel-shaped blade and antler bone handle."

"How much?" Edwin asked, unsheathing the knife and thumbing the blade's edge. It was sharp as all hell and a suitable fit for his grasp.

"That's one of a kind," said the fur trader. "Ten dollars."

"Would you take five?" Edwin countered.

"Fuck no…But I might take eight," the fur trader counter-countered.

Edwin felt the sturdiness of the knife in his hand. "With the sheath?"

"Ay," the fur trader said.

"I'll take it for seven," Edwin proclaimed. The fur trader agreed with a nod. Edwin snuck notes from his newly seized billfold, then exited wearing the knife on his belt, feeling mightier as he slung the sack of provisions over his shoulder and strutted toward Summer Street.

It was early evening when he got back to the shop, and although he had the provisions for a trip, he still did not have the destination. Edwin went up to his loft, rolled a cigarette, and packed his pantry goods in with his sacked provisions. He knew all of his clothing would fit into the trunk by the foot of the cot but didn't know where he was going to put the trunk. He no longer had enough funds to line up a cart, let alone the horse, and he couldn't be dragging a trunk around if he was going to be on foot or having to switch trains. He decided that the best approach would be to bring along only what he could carry.

An hour later, Edwin had managed to whittle down his belongings into one satchel and a duffle bag. It was as sad as it was efficient. All packed up with nowhere to go, Edwin stuffed charcoal and graphite bits into his pocket, rolled another cigarette, took a hearty gulp of vodka, then shouldered his bags and headed downstairs.

The blackness of night had snuck up outside, and Edwin could barely see the shop as he took one last slightly remorseful look at it. Just then, something stirred in one of the shadowed corners. "Who's there?" Edwin barked.

A match struck and lit a cigarette that revealed Strickland's bruised and busted face with its glow. "Don't worry, beefer. It's only me…" Strickland said with a snarl, using the last bit of the match to light a candle lantern on a table nearby, eerily illuminating the room.

"My terms with Wilkinson are to be out by midnight…It's just eight now," Edwin said assuredly, hiding the slight tremble in his voice.

"I don't give a two-bit whore's fuck about yer terms," Strickland growled as he paced closer. "I'm here pro rata ya tamping up my face, ya cheap-shot-throwing scrap of afterbirth."

"You deserved it and more. I ain't sorry," Edwin stated, holding his ground.

"You will be," Strickland replied menacingly, pulling a knife from his waist. "My papi gave me that piece ya tossed in the harbor, so now I'll just have to stab ya to death."

Edwin grit his teeth. Thinking fast, he threw his duffle bag at Strickland to distract his approach. Strickland deflected the bag, but it was too late. Edwin pulled out his knife and launched it into Strickland's gut with a grotesque-sounding squish. Strickland's eyes went wild, face to face with Edwin's equally wild and startled gaze. Strickland took a weak swipe with his own blade now, but Edwin blocked it, using Strickland's momentum to spike the swung knife back up under his chin and into his head. Strickland bobbled, trying to grip at both of the knives put into him. Edwin stepped back, watching Strickland fall to his knees and bleed profusely from the wounds. Life slipped away from Strickland's eyes as his body slumped to the ground.

Edwin knelt near the spreading pool of blood, vomiting with disgust. He had never killed a man, and now had done so in the shop he grew up in. He didn't have the same wash of adrenaline felt after fisticuffs with Strickland the day before. Taking his life seemed entirely more permanent than Edwin had time to reckon with. Although the shock of it all weighed heavily on Edwin's mind, he needed to escape now. He exfoliated meager comfort from the fact that he'd acted in self-defense.

Strickland's body leaked onto the floor; it was beginning to grow sour. Edwin set his bags by the door, then carefully retrieved his shiny new knife from the gut of Strickland's corpse. It was not so shiny and new anymore. Edwin knew Mr. Wilkinson would not appreciate finding his lapdog stuck and drained on the floor when he arrived to claim the acquired property at midnight. Edwin would have to dispose of the body, but how was he supposed to pull that off if he couldn't even dispose of a trunk locker? For just a moment, the thought of coming clean with the authorities crossed Edwin's mind. As if the law would ever believe his side of the story. More likely, he presumed, he'd end up charged with murder and tossed in lockup for the rest of his able-bodied years. *To hell with that,* Edwin thought in a panic. *Get the fuck out of here.*

Edwin dug money out of Strickland's wallet, then did the only thing he could think of to cover his tracks—tipping over the lantern and letting it spark across boot material fibers on the floor. Flames caught and kicked up all around, igniting the corner of Strickland's trousers. Edwin stood by the door with a mix of shock and excitement as the flames danced in the reflection of his pupils. The rest of Strickland's body caught now, along with the wooden worktables. The fire was spreading onto the walls and climbed up to the ceiling with a crackling roar. Edwin grabbed his luggage and left the shop in a hurry.

The fire was now visible from across the street, if anyone was looking. The storefront glass broke under the pressure and wood beams crackled as they split. The Morris Shoemaking Company banner caught now and flamed away from its hooks for good. Edwin turned his back, marching off with quickness, jaw clenched with fear and exhilaration. It was nearing 9 p.m., which meant the train station wouldn't be open until morning and Edwin would need to find somewhere to bunk down for the night. He couldn't waste money on a hotel, but he also couldn't risk staying on the street. He then remembered a hidden crawlspace under one of the wharfs that he used to explore as a kid and went for the docks.

The harbor was damp, dim, and foggy. All the shops were closed, and anyone who had come down there otherwise would have been in the pubs or brothels two blocks over. Edwin hopped over a barrier onto the pier leading to the Francis Wharf. The docks were deserted except for one group of workers staying busy at the end of the slip, which was near the crawlspace Edwin planned on bunking down in. He quietly moved closer for a better look.

A hardened-looking faction of seamen heaved supplies onto a massive ship—a far-reaching vessel with a wide hull and large masts. A broad man with grey hair, a blue wool slicker, and a hardened presence oversaw everything from the deck of the ship. Edwin assumed him to be the captain, and then stretched his gaze across the dock toward another stoic bloke with a ledger herding the sailors. Thrusting solely on impulse, Edwin rethought his plans and approached the man, who he would later learn was the first mate named Robinson. "Good evening," Edwin said with a cautious optimism. "Pushing off tomorrow?"

"Pushing tonight," Robinson said without turning around. "Who wants to know?"

"My name is Morris. Are you in need of crew?" Edwin asked, trying not to sound too much like a mooch, knowing that far-reaching vessels were always in need of crew. Trade ships were known for high turnover rates, as sailors were constantly injured or quit without notice. It was a rough-and-tumble occupation that most men were not cut out for. Robinson turned to face Edwin, judging his stature with unimpressed eyes.

"You look like a young shit. Ever work at sea before?" Robinson said.

"Never. But I'm not afraid of hard labor," Edwin said with a defiant conviction. "Formally a cobbler. I'm good with tools and textiles."

"Your rags are more suited for a funeral than a ship."

"I came from a funeral just yesterday," Edwin said, without even a hint of irony.

Robinson scanned Edwin's bags and muted demeanor once more, noticing a bit of blood on his sleeve and stains of sweat browning his collar. "Running from something?"

"Just need a change of place and a job, sir," Edwin said.

Robinson thought on it for a moment. "We're sailing around Cape Horn to San Francisco before turning back. A month at sea will break most men, let alone a year."

"I can handle it," Edwin said proudly, not actually sure if he could or not.

"Wages are paid upon completion of the run. You'd be in it for the long haul…Pays a thousand dollars per man, plus room and board along the way."

"I can accept those terms," Edwin agreed, thinking he'd most likely jump ship in San Francisco. He might not get paid, but at least he'd get transport to the west coast, and more importantly, this escape vessel was leaving tonight. Edwin had no problem bartering his labor for passage, even if this new employer wasn't in on the deal.

"Check in with Kersey. He's the black fella on deck over there," Robinson said, pointing forward. "Drop your packs off and fall in line. We push at midnight." Robinson returned to overwatch and dismissed Edwin with the pivot.

"Yes, sir, thank you, sir," Edwin said as he scuttled by, still wrestling with the ringing in his head that had been sounding off since killing Strickland.

"One more thing," Robinson added. "Don't make me hate you. You fuck around or can't hold your own, and you'll be left at sea. Gots no tolerance for chum scrubbers hitching a ride without merit. Ay?"

"Ay," Edwin said assuredly, as if used to the lingo. He lugged his bags over his shoulders and approached the ship with curiosity. It was impressive, with three looming masts and square maroon sails. A thick white stripe stretched along the circumference of its thick oak hull, otherwise painted black. The crew was loading bound crates of cargo onto the deck with ropes and pulleys. Edwin found Kersey, a sturdy-looking African American with sideburns and wide shoulders. "Edwin Morris, reporting for duty," he said with sincerity.

"Says who?" Kersey blasted in return, busy with securing a rope.

"That man there offered me a position. I'm to stow my packs and fall in," Edwin said, pointing to Robinson. Kersey turned his gaze to find Robinson nodding approval.

"Okay. Drop your packs; we'll stow 'em later. Need to get this cargo hitched," Kersey said with the same *I don't have time for this shit* demeanor Robinson employed.

"Understood," Edwin said. He dropped his bags and removed his jacket, rolling up his sleeves to fall in and help other crewmen pack and load crates. It was laborious work lifting and loading the cargo, and most of the crew paid Edwin no mind. He was just another ordinary seaman wet behind the ears to them, worthless until proven otherwise. Edwin pitched in with every crate, working for hours before anyone even made eye contact with him. Once the last crate was loaded, Kersey returned to fetch him.

"Newcomer!" Kersey said, pointing at Edwin. "Grab your shit. On my hip."

"Ay," Edwin said, snatching his bags and following Kersey on to the main deck.

"The name's Kersey. Morgan Kersey."

"Edwin Morris," Edwin replied, reaching out to shake hands firmly.

"Good to meet ya, Ed. First time at sea?"

"It is, but I'm a fast learner and eager to prove my work ethic."

"We'll see…Watch your head," Kersey said, just in time, helping Edwin to avoid a pulley beam getting boomed over the side. "Best to keep those eyes wide, Mr. Morris."

"Seems so. Obliged," Edwin said, somewhat embarrassed.

"Welcome to the Salty Mariner," Kersey said with a dry wit. The main deck was wide, slippery, and packed to its brim with the ship's structure and cargo. The masts stretched into the sky. It was tough for Edwin to navigate for the first time at night. Kersey led him below the quarterdeck into the ship's galley, currently getting stocked by two AB sailors under yelling orders of the chief cook, who was too busy to introduce himself. From there, Kersey and Edwin slinked through a joiner door and went below deck further, to the general crew quarters. It was a squatted compartment packed full of bunk beds. Sconce lanterns put off an orange glow and outlined a permanent layer of cigar smoke that surrounded a few sailors in the corner playing cards before their night shift began. It smelled like piss, smoke, wood, and all the worst body odors, and it was Edwin's new home.

"Take that bottom bunk to the left," Kersey said, pointing it out. "Drop your shit, then I'll introduce you to some folks on deck before we push off."

Edwin nodded and did as he was told, following Kersey back up to the main deck.

"Your shift starts at sunrise," Kersey explained, showing Edwin through the waist of the upper deck. "Report to the boatswain on duty at the time—it's Foster tomorrow, I believe."

"What is your rank and duties?" Edwin asked.

"I'm a senior AB, on my way to boatswain soon enough, though."

Edwin nodded with a vacant expression like he understood, not wanting to appear to be green. But Kersey saw right through him, all too familiar with cocky green OS claiming to be seasoned AB. Kersey cut him some slack, though, and led him through a breakdown of the ship's hierarchy as they leaned against the starboard rail. "You're an OS right now," Kersey said, laying it all out. "That's the lowest class. Above that are AB like me who take orders from the boatswain, who take orders from the ship mates taking orders from the captain."

"Right…" Edwin said with the same vacantly expressed nod.

"You'll get it. Just keep yer ears and eyes open and work yer ass off."

"That, I can do," Edwin replied, scanning the deck and all the different jobs being performed to get the ship ready for pushing off. OS and AB secured cargo and housed any equipment not being used, while the boatswain on duty double-checked a manifest and doled out additional tasks. The controlled chaos of it all intrigued Edwin's tinkering mind.

That is, until he noticed some fellas coming toward him that he recognized from town.

"Well, speak of the devil," Kersey said of the two meatheads that robbed Edwin the night before—now strolling right up to them. Neither meathead seemed to recognize Edwin, but Edwin couldn't forget either of them, no matter how shit-faced drunk he'd been. "This is Blake Mathews and Joe Banyan," Kersey said. "Our illustrious second and third mates."

No fucking shit, Ed thought. "Good to meet you," he said.

The taller meathead was Mathews and the shorter one was Banyan. Edwin's gut turned, but he played along, not wanting to let on to his recognition or stir up any beef with who were now, apparently, his superiors. "You look like a coupl'a mop-Mary's on the bum, just standing there," Mathews barked with a sloppy disparagement. "Who the fuck is this, anyway?" he added, pointing to Edwin.

"Morris," Edwin said, extending his hand. Mathews huffed, staring Edwin up and down while disregarding the handshake.

"Looks like a young shit," Banyan said. Edwin stared blankly and bit his tongue.

"Seems like fair winds tonight," Kersey said, changing the subject to break tension.

"You both off duty or getting paid to lean?" Mathews said, keeping on topic.

"Off duty 'til morning for the newcomer. My watch starts at 2 a.m.," Kersey replied.

"Fine," Mathews huffed as he and Banyan carried on. Edwin looked to Kersey like, *Fuck those guys*, and Kersey agreed with a *yer damn right* smirk of his own.

"Coupl'a fucks, those two," Kersey said. "They take their orders only from Robinson, who is Captain Renault's eyes, ears, and mouthpiece, as far as you're concerned. Shit rolls downhill from there to me and you and all the other mopes you'll be bunking up with."

Robinson, with Captain Renault looming over his shoulder, leaned across the tiller and began barking orders at the boatswain on deck. "Drop the sails and unhitch the ties, you bindle punks! We're setting sail!" Robinson's commands threw the crew into a beehive of activity. The anchors were yanked out of the water and the sails dropped rhythmically into position. The hull creaked against the pier as the ship pushed off.

"Right on time," Kersey said, checking his pocket watch.

"It's midnight already?" Edwin asked.

"Indeed," Kersey replied. "We're dog shit if we don't keep up with the manifest. You should have seen the one time we were just three days late and the trading company owner lost it. Straight up hollered in Renault's face for damn near half an hour, then held back our wages. Eight-month run with no coin to show for it. I mean, Renault is a villainous fuck, but the owner of this here enterprise is the real shit-kicker you don't wanna quarrel with."

"Who is the owner? Is he onboard?" Edwin asked.

"Never. He manages the fleet from headquarters. Nasty bastard named Wilkinson."

"No shit..." Edwin said with a callous surprise, now realizing he had wandered on to one of Mr. Wilkinson's trading ships.

"You know him?"

"I almost married his daughter," Edwin said, hoping to sum it up there.

"No shit..." Kersey replied, more to himself, shaking his head with a chuckle. Edwin leaned against the rail, staring back at the harbor as it got further away. In the distance, he could see an orange glow kicking up under black, pluming smoke near Summer Street. The fire he set was spreading. It would later be known as the Great Boston Fire—charring nearly seventy acres in its wake. Edwin couldn't have known the damage it would cause, but he also couldn't have cared any less. Without Lillian, there was nothing left for him in Boston, and now her father was again paying for him to leave it all behind—an irony not lost on Edwin as he watched the flames scatter. A strong wind caught the sails and pushed the Salty Mariner out to sea. Edwin stared across the port side rail, silently saying goodbye to the only home he had ever known.

4

BEARING SOUTH

"Is that the family tomb yonder where the yews grow so thick?"
was the unexpected reply to her question, and she turned to look at
her, not at all daunted by her manner.

"Yes, and that reminds me to ask you why you
were napping there, instead of doing your errands."

"I leaped the fence and strained to look about me, and enjoy
myself, Miss Hester" was the air of drawing, and she could not help a
laugh as he confessed his trespass.

"You look as if you'd had a long walk. Where do you come from?
London?"

"Bless the boy! It's fifty miles away."

"So my shoes show, but it's a pleasant trip."

"But why did you walk, child, had you no money?"

"Plenty, but not for wasting. I wanted to see if my own
legs could carry me, and look, two days' holiday and
for little..."

"... that, and Hester gave a little approving
nod as if that's your way of spending holi...
...now you are sufficiently rested, I'll pro...
please, for she is already ill."

"...Sir Richard...
...ago was that...
...or more."

"...young gen...

"No...

"A proud...

"And well she...
than the Treylyns, and she...

"Is that the Treylyn coat of arms," asked the young man,
pointing to a stone falcon with the motto...
over the gate through which they were just...

"Yes. Why do you ask?"

"Mere curiosity; I know something of heraldry, and learn
these things for my own pleasure. One learns...
abroad," he added, seeing an expression of sur...
face.

"You'll have little time for study here this..."
"...to the keeper, and if you're wise you'll ask no...
of him, for you'll get no answer."

The Salty Mariner cruised steadily through the Atlantic Ocean while making her way down the east coast of America. The general quarters were shadowed in tobacco smoke, with the other AB on morning shift already milling about as Edwin plopped out of bed to make an attempt at composing himself for the day. He hadn't slept well at all that first night onboard. Visions of Strickland's final moments haunted his mind between agonizing despair over Lillian and the shop and the realization that he had really just enlisted for a year at sea, on the run, with less than one hundred dollars to his name. Not to mention puking into a bucket from seasickness throughout the night, much to the annoyance of his more seasoned colleagues trying to sleep off their hangovers before work.

"Just go kill yourself already, Angelina!" one of the AB barked.

"Fuckin' dummy!" another added. It was far from a crack first impression, from which Edwin knew he'd have to redeem himself. He refused to be deemed useless, and certainly didn't need any help from seasickness and nightmares. *Get your shit together*, Edwin thought, throwing on slacks and boots before following the other morning shift AB out.

The galley was a decent-sized compartment in width but featured a low ceiling not at all suitable for a tall and lanky shit like Edwin. Cargo nets full of produce and canned goods lined the walls, with slim wooden tables and benches shoved down the middle, leading to a corner cook station that the chief cook barely managed to fit himself into. He was a large man, fat not bulky, with a sour bearded mug, dirty clothes, and a derby hat a size too small. No one knew his real name and most of the crew just called him Chief or CK—as the galley was referred to as Chief's Kitchen. CK chewed on a cigar and sat on a stool within the cook station. To his left was a small cabinet of pots and pans that had a countertop for prepping food and a modest spice rack mounted to the side of it. To his right was a wood fire stove with four burners in a row that were all in use. There was a bread maker on the main deck as well, but CK rarely felt like walking up there to tend to it, which meant bread only got made once or twice a week at best, and it usually wasn't enough for everyone to get some.

Edwin got in line with other AB, all yawing and stretching, making their way up to the cook station to be handed a bowl of slop and a mug of coffee. Breakfast today consisted of a scoop of runny eggs and a boiled potato with too much salt. Most AB accepted it as the standard ship mush, but

Edwin was actually quite delighted to have a hot breakfast for once. Especially one he didn't have to cook. The coffee was total shit, though—watery, full of grinds, and it was barely warm. Edwin choked it down and dug into his meal. Most AB nodded silently as they sat down along the benches, but many didn't even bother sitting. They slurped their coffee and eggs standing up near the counter, then ditched the bowls and went up to the main deck fisting a potato to chew on along the way. "You the newcomer been puking all night," one of the younger AB said to Edwin, sitting across from him at the table.

"I suppose so…Apologies," Edwin said, figuring it was just another rub.

"That was me on my first go of it," the AB continued, in a much friendlier tone than Edwin had been expecting. "Feels like you'll never fucking sleep again at first, but you do get used to it," he said with a nod, then went on to introduce himself as Sam Barton. He was a scrappy fella in his late twenties, with an easy way about him. His father was a sailing man and so naturally Sam was to be a sailing man too. He had spent his whole life on boats and joined the Salty Mariner crew just last year. "You on morning shift?" Sam asked.

"I am," Edwin replied.

"I can show ya some stuff, if ya like?" Sam said as he bit a potato in half with one bite and stood to leave. Edwin followed suit, discarding his bowl and coffee mug to a bin full of them in the corner. Sam nudged Edwin like, *Check this out*, then got CK's attention.

"Hey there, Chief. What's for dinner tonight?" Sam asked.

"Mulligan stew," CK said with a grunt.

"How about tomorrow night?"

"Mulligan stew."

"And the night after that?"

"Go fuck yourself," CK said, annoyed with the familiar routine. Sam laughed and waved on, leading Edwin up to the main deck to report for duty. The wind was cold but somewhat calm; the sun was cresting over the eastern horizon, sending streaks of hotspots across the rippling waves. Edwin froze for a moment near the rails, not prepared for how serene and picturesque the view would be. It gave him the much-needed hit of exhilaration that the coffee had left him without. Walt Foster was the boatswain on duty, just as Kersey had said. Foster was a statuesque seasoned sailor hiding in plain sight, wearing black boots, a wool cap, and a leather slicker. Edwin went to introduce himself but was met with a stern glare that said, *I don't give a fuck.*

Tasks were doled out promptly. Edwin and Sam spent the rest of that morning scrubbing the deck with long-handled mops. Every day, the deck had to be scrubbed with water and solvent to keep the wood from cracking and rotting. It was hard work, but it was also a welcome change from the aimless squatted fussing Edwin had gotten used to back home. He thought about the chain of events that led him here, wishing he could have at least seen the speechless look on Mr. Wilkinson's cloddish, smug fuck of a face when he learned what happened to his lapdog and charred new real estate investment. It was nearing noon now, and Edwin felt like he was getting away with something. There was nothing Mr. Wilkinson, or anyone back in Boston, could do to him out at sea. It was a freeing feeling, followed immediately by the un-freeing feeling of breakfast twisting ferociously within his bowels. Edwin dropped the mop handle, nearly barreling over. "Where's the shitter?" he yelled.

"Head's in the bow," Sam said, pointing with a slightly maniacal grin. Edwin nodded like he knew what the bow was and made his way down to the head compartment at the front of the ship. He squatted over a wooden box-like tube that opened into a chamber below. Vented slots allowed ocean waves to sweep in and clear out the waste. There were two seats facing each other and Edwin was glad not to have some other bloke squatting across the way staring back at him. *This is my life now*, he thought as a wave crashed into the compartment below and splashed waste back up the toilets, peppering Edwin in the ass and across his boots…*Fuck me.*

Back at the galley, lunch was a bowl of tough beans and soggy cabbage. Edwin sat next to Sam and the rest of the AB from morning shift shoveling their grub down. They were a tough-looking bunch with names like Geno and Collins and Dudley and Maurice, ranging in age and ethnicity but all hardened in some way by their lives at sea. Staring at their weathered faces, Edwin imagined how some might be running from their past too, or that others might just be drifting to avoid their future. Most AB would warm up to the point of being cordial after a week or two, but many wouldn't even bother to look at Edwin, let alone introduce themselves. Despite that, Edwin felt more at ease with these miscreant strangers than he had with most folks back home. Of course, thinking about back home always made Edwin's mind wander back to Lillian. He still ached with missing her touch, her laugh, and the way that her hair smelled like spring. Edwin mulled over it all as he slopped up the rest of his beans.

Then Banyan plodded into the galley, instantly pulling Edwin from his idle pondering. The mates and boatswains had their own quarters near the aft of the ship, just under the captain's quarters in the cockpit. Banyan cut the line of AB waiting and fetched two trays of slightly less soggy, slightly heartier portions of grub CK had set aside to take back to their private eating compartment. "You or one yer galley bitches is supposed to bring the trays," Banyan barked at CK. "I ain't gon' be playing fetch no more." CK just shrugged and waved Banyan off.

That motherfucker poached me, Edwin thought over and over, wanting to scream it at the top of his lungs while aiming his dagger accusingly. He'd need to contain his emotions for now, though, especially if any revenge was to be plotted. Mathews and Banyan not knowing Edwin's true identity was his best-kept secret. That is, aside from the whole *murdering Strickland and setting a fire to cover it up* incident. Edwin wasn't holding out hope for getting his money back but desperately wanted to find out if Banyan still had Lillian's harmonica.

"Ready for more punches?" Sam said, breaking Edwin's train of thought.

"Might as well be," Edwin replied.

"Ay," Sam said with a friendly nod, then continued on to lead Edwin through a crash course of duties for the rest of the day. They scrubbed algae off the anchors, which had collected while being docked in Boston, checked over the bilge and removed standing water, secured cargo in the stores and shifted pallets for better weight distribution, then cleaned the galley and washed all the day's dishes. Edwin tried to roll a cigarette up on the main deck during a quick break between tasks, but the wind made it nearly impossible. Sam had a good laugh over it, then handed over a pre-rolled cigarette to ease the distraction. "Do yourself a favor and roll a few down below before your shift. Not likely to find too many fair winds until we get around Cape Horn. And even then," Sam said.

Edwin thanked Sam for his guidance while lighting both of their smokes, struggling now to strike a match in the wind as well. Through strife, they enjoyed every pull of those cigarettes before getting back to work. All the while, Edwin kept an eye on Mathews and Banyan, jabbering to themselves between shots of whiskey and barking orders to the boatswains. Edwin hated them, which seemed to be the general consensus from most of the other AB too, based on the rolling eyes and annoyed grunts offered behind their backs every time they'd pass by.

Dinner marked the end of day shift, and Edwin welcomed the lukewarm clam and onion soup that was served. The galley was crowded with a mix of day shifters getting off duty and night shifters just starting their day. Edwin felt he was getting eyeballed for taking up a seat by some of the older, meaner-looking night crew standing in the corner, so he did not linger.

AB were free to wander the deck when not on duty, so long as they didn't get in the way. Most men drank and rested up or played cards in quarters. Edwin grabbed a bottle of bourbon from his duffle bag under his bunk and came across an old book tucked away by the last sorry sack that slept there. It was a decently bound copy of Louisa May Alcott's dime novel *The Mysterious Key*. Edwin didn't give a damn about reading it but was excited for the pages it was printed on. He put the book into his pocket and snaked out the hallway passage with the bourbon.

A hearty gust carried the Salty Mariner through the fog of night. Her sails billowed out in unison and made a soothing yet ominous flapping sound every time the winds shifted. Edwin took sips of bourbon while leaning over the starboard quarterdeck rail, getting lost in the thick sea of blackness the ship was cruising through below him. After gazing off for a few moments, Edwin stood straight and turned his back, not wanting to get caught looking like some kind of starry-eyed green idiot. Nor did he want to appear to be a Nancy-boy artist as he put graphite to the pages of *The Mysterious Key*. In small snuck bursts, he drew an abstract outline of the ship's sails over the book's writing.

"Ya scribbling a journal, or what kind of Nancy-boy shit ya doin' there, Morris?" Kersey said with a crinkled face as he approached. He was starting night shift rounds and thought it appropriate to come give Edwin some shit when he saw him leaning over the corner rail like some starry-eyed green idiot.

"Just some drawing. Sort of a hobby," Edwin said, feeling busted and snapping the book closed. "Never mind, you wouldn't understand."

"Black folks know what art is too, tramp."

"That's not what I meant," Edwin said, feeling even more embarrassed.

"I'm fucking with you. Lemme see it," Kersey said. Edwin handed the book over shyly. Kersey took a look and simply nodded his head. "Old salty never looked so good," he said. "So how was day one?"

"So far so well," Edwin replied. "Care for a nip?" he added, offering the bourbon.

"Shit, yeah." Kersey took a healthy swig.

"Where ya from?" Edwin asked, taking the bottle and book back.

"Virginia," Kersey said proudly.

"I've never been. Is it nice?"

"It's not without some nice aspects," Kersey joked, going on to explain that his parents met on a plantation in Georgia, then moved north to Virginia after the war. He was the first man in his family born into freedom after the Emancipation Proclamation and found his way onto a trade ship at fifteen when it was the only work he could secure as a young man looking to earn a real living. There was still a stigma with hiring black men in prominently white towns for anything but shit service jobs, and he wouldn't be satisfied working as a manor butler or stable boy. Ships always needed crew and, although they were indeed a tempestuous group of boozers and delinquents, sailors cooperated with all walks of life so long as a fella busted his ass. Kersey stayed with it over the years and was well on his way to becoming a journeyman sailor. He didn't mind hard work and could get along with almost anyone. Much like Edwin, he craved adventure and purpose. "Figure if I keep working hard, then one day I'll be running my own ship. Plus, I ain't nobody's nigger out here, know what I mean?" Kersey said.

"I believe I do," Edwin replied.

"Good. Then I don't have to repeat myself," Kersey said. "So, what's your story?"

Edwin went on to tell Kersey about his simple upbringing, and his mother and uncle passing, then about his father, and the shop, and Lillian's passing, and the whole sloping chain of events that transpired into Edwin landing onboard the Salty Mariner in the middle of the night before. Edwin did not, however, mention killing Strickland or setting the fire, and although he told Kersey about getting mugged, he did not include the fact that it was the Salty Mariner's second and third mates who were responsible.

"That's a hell of a run, Ed," Kersey exhaled.

"Not the end of it, I hope," Edwin reaffirmed to himself more than to Kersey. The bourbon bottle was empty now, and both of them had a pretty good buzz going. Kersey checked his pocket watch as Edwin let out a slow, rumbling belch.

"Suppose I oughta get to my rounds now, and you might wanna get some shuteye. Heard a bloke was puking his fucking guts out last night…guessing that was you?" Kersey said. Edwin nodded and shrugged. "Don't think so much," Kersey added. "You'll be fine."

"That should not be a problem. It was good speaking with you," Edwin said.

"Rest easy, Morris. I've got some scotch for next time." Kersey twirled his pocket watch and strolled off with a nod. Edwin took one last gaze into the waves crashing against the ship before heading toward the quarterdeck ladder leading below. Then a sound hit Edwin's ears that stopped him dead in his tracks—a sound he was both eager and angry to hear all at once. It was a harmonica being played…badly. Edwin tracked the tune through the waist of the ship and peered behind a supply crate toward the stern. Banyan stood there playing Lillian's harmonica. Edwin caught himself snarling, instinctually gripping at the knife handle on his hip and wanting to march over and slit Banyan's goddamn thieving throat. Edwin hadn't even played the harmonica once himself, and there it was in Banyan's grimy digits with his fat swamper lips mouth-fucking the piss out of it. Edwin took a heavy gulp and drunken steps forward, pulling the knife halfway out of the sheath. Just then, Mathews stumbled over to Banyan like a sloth with a shit-faced expression slapped across his jowls.

"Cut that shit out!" Mathews barked drunkenly.

"I'll never get any good if you fuckers don't let me play it!" Banyan quipped with a pout, pulling the harmonica off his stinky choppers and shoving it in his coat.

"No one's askin' ya to get good! Just toss that fuckin' noise box over," Mathews slurred.

"Fuck that. You'll see. I'll get goddamn great at it, despite you!" Banyan slurred back. Edwin let his knife ease back into its sheath and hid in the shadows, watching the two idiots drunkenly debate the merits of Banyan learning how to play the harmonica or not. Edwin's mind raced. He couldn't confront Banyan while outnumbered at sea, but at least he now knew that the harmonica was in range. He'd have to let it be for now, and come up with a plan that didn't jeopardize his transport.

The bourbon was catching up to Edwin as he made his way below deck to the crew quarters. A few AB were still playing poker by lantern light in the corner as Edwin kicked off his boots and sank into his bunk, managing to pass out for a while before the next morning snuck up.

Edwin woke with a nasty headache. He rolled three cigarettes and stuffed them in his vest pocket before throwing on his boots. The next several days went much like the first. The sea was calm. Edwin worked with Sam and the other AB during the day, and would draw and drink at night. He was getting the hang of his duties and had made acquaintances on the ship, but with Sam and Kersey he'd become something close to friends. The three of them met for drinks at night, exchanging stories from home and pining for indulgences they were left without at sea.

One morning a few weeks in, Edwin woke early with a particularly throbbing, moonshine-induced headache. He dug out the percolator and coffee tin from his duffle bag and marched out of the quarters, determined to get a strong cup of coffee. He had never gone so long without it before, and the lack of caffeine was taking its toll. Edwin entered the galley before the morning shift rush and marched up to CK at the serving counter. "Any chance you could spare a burner?"

"The fuck for?" CK barked back.

"For a decent goddamn cup of java. That lukewarm shit you serve tastes like it came from a sock."

"Maybe it did. Maybe fuck you," CK said, crossing his arms.

"Come on now. You can have some as well. I've got quality grinds here," Edwin said, handing the preloaded percolator halfway over the counter and hoping CK wouldn't backhand it away just to make Edwin clean it all up.

"Fine," CK said, "but you's gotta deliver breakfast to the mates' quarters."

"Deal," Edwin said. "Any day of the week, that's a goddamn deal." CK took the percolator and plopped it onto the one spare burner, then loaded several bowls of grub onto trays. Breakfast today was burnt sausage floating in the leftover soup from last night's dinner. Edwin leveled the trays in his hands and went on toward the mates' quarters near the stern. Not only would he soon have a real cup of coffee, but he was now being given an opportunity to scout the mates' quarters without having to masquerade. Edwin aimed to find out where Banyan slept and kept the harmonica. He reached the mates' quarters and found Robinson, Mathews, Banyan, and Foster all sitting around a small table next to their slightly more spacious gallery of bunks. At first annoyed by an AB entering their quarters, they quickly became civil upon realizing Edwin had brought breakfast and wasn't just there to pester them before a shift. Edwin placed the trays on the table, playing off his contempt for Banyan and Mathews with a cordial front.

"Better still be hot," Banyan said.

Go fuck yourself, Edwin thought. "Right off the stove," he said instead. The mates all grabbed a bowl and utensils, then dismissed Edwin with the trays, leaving one bowl left for delivery to Captain Renault. Edwin carefully eyed each bunk on his way out, trying to decipher which one could be Banyan's. It was hard to tell, but Edwin thought he recognized a coat and hat combo he saw Banyan wear earlier hanging on a hook by the closest bunk to the door. Edwin noted the layout, sure to leave without lingering too long.

The next compartment over was Captain Renault's private quarters. Edwin knocked firmly on the closed door. "Captain, sir, I have your breakfast here. If interested," he said.

"Bring it in, then," Renault hollered from inside. Edwin opened the door and entered the spacious cabin. A sizeable bed lined the wall next to built-in cabinets and a personal commode. Renault sat behind a large oak desk covered in maps and manifests. Galley windows let the first bit of morning light sneak over his shoulder and outline the puffs of smoke kicking up from his pipe. This was the first time Edwin got a good look at his captain. Renault had bright-white hair and deep pores and wrinkles that outlined his harsh sea salt-blasted expressions. He was sharp as a tack, angry as all hell, and still stout and agile for a man closer to sixty years old than he was to fifty. Edwin had learned from others that Renault cut his sailing teeth as a young man working schooners on coastal runs up, down, and between every shipyard on the eastern seaboard. He was a decorated veteran of the Civil War, captaining steam frigate war vessels for the Union out of the Charlestown Navy Yard before entering the private sector where his allegiances could fetch more profit. Renault ran the ship as though she were a military operation and was always a real fucking bastard about it. "Better still be hot," Renault said.

"Right off the stove, sir," Edwin said in service, placing the grub like a chef presenting his dish in a South Boston cafe. Renault stuffed a cloth napkin down his collar and readied a spoon. He glared at Edwin, sneering instead of saying, *You may go now.*

"Yes, sir," Edwin replied, retracting the tray and turning to leave just as—*BLAM*—a wave blasted the ship's broad side with a loud, crackling howl that echoed and trembled. Edwin fell over and Renault nearly ended up with a face full of mush as the Salty Mariner swayed violently, then rumbled back into a recovery.

On the main deck, Edwin could hear an AB ringing the warning bell as fast as he could. "All hands on deck!" the boatswain yelled between rings.

Renault grabbed his slicker and bolted from the cabin, knocking Edwin back over as he passed. Edwin just managed to get to his feet when—*BLAM*—another wave knocked against the port side, jerking the ship with a roar. Edwin held himself up as shelves emptied all around. He ran from the cabin and veered through the narrow passages out. Water washed itself down the hallway as Edwin hopped up the forecastle ladder and made his way to the upper deck. *BLAM*— another wave hit, sending a punch of water across the ship's deck just as Edwin arrived. Most crew braced, but Edwin was hit by the wave and sent hard into the side rail. Water blasted by, pinning him back until it passed. The ship's bearing shifted, and Edwin slid out of control across the deck toward the stern, where Renault and Robinson were fighting for control of the wheel within what was developing into a large gale windstorm. Robinson flexed the wheel against the current. Renault held on to a rope swung around the mizzenmast, barking orders. "Swing toward the next one! Point her right away!" he yelled at the top of his hoary olden lungs.

"I'm trying!" Robinson yelled back.

"Get the fuck out of my way, then!" Renault shoved Robinson aside to grip the wheel handles himself. Robinson fell back and slid into Edwin.

"What the fuck are you doing up here?" he yelled while colliding with Edwin.

"I don't know!" Edwin yelled back, trying to get to his feet.

"Secure the main deck, moper! Move!" Robinson heaved Edwin forward.

Lightning cackled around the ship and left rolling thunder in its wake, bringing with it a thick, heavy rain that soaked the sky. Edwin ran along the port side, weaving between AB getting to their stations. The bell rang again, and a boatswain yelled out, "Brace!"

"Hold onto something, rum-dum!" Kersey said, appearing just in time to grab on to Edwin and push him toward the rail. *BLAM*—the ship hit a wave dead on. Water shot across the bow and rinsed the main deck. Edwin and Kersey held on until the rushing water passed by. *SNAP*—the middle mount on the foremast broke free and ripped away above their heads, tearing a sail from its beams. "Get to the bow!" Kersey shouted over the wind. Edwin moved forward, keeping his balance as the ship pivoted below his feet, joining up with Sam and other AB huddled by the foremast.

"Edwin!" Sam yelled over the wind. "With me! Hope yer not afraid of heights."

"What's the plan?" Edwin yelled back.

"We've got to cut that busted wing loose or it's gonna tear the rest to shreds!" Sam said with adrenaline pumping, getting ready to climb up the service nets mounted to the foremast with two other appointed AB. "Let's get on with it," he added sternly.

Edwin followed Sam's lead, climbing up a thick rope net toward the busted middle sail still fifty feet above their heads. The wind blew heartier the higher they climbed. Edwin gripped the soaked and swaying net, struggling to keep up with Sam and the others more used to such tasks. They were halfway up when the warning bell rang out again from the deck below.

"Brace!" one of the AB hollered out.

"Hold on!" Sam squawked at Edwin. *BLAM*—a wave blasted across the bow of the ship, overtaking the main deck with water and striking Edwin, Sam, and the other AB climbing up the nets. The ship swayed, with the masts whipping across the sky. Edwin's feet slipped off the net, but he managed to hang on with his hands, doing a ninety-degree extension that flailed his feet nearly horizontal with the water below until the ship resurrected her balance.

Edwin lurched against the foremast net, barely hanging on. He pulled himself tight against the ropes as wind and water slapped his back. Sam held tight to the other side of the net, shaking his head with a grin. "Onward!" he yelled to Edwin and the other AB. They heaved themselves further up the nets and finally arrived near the top at the broken sail mounts, eighty feet up above the frantic main deck below. Ropes were snagged to the broken sail ripping in the wind, yanking more mounts loose in its struggle. "We need to cut those free!" Sam yelled, pointing to the tangled ropes.

Edwin wielded his knife and followed suit, climbing out on to the crossbeam next to Sam while the other AB worked on securing a loose mount a few feet below them. The warning bell sounded off once again, giving Edwin chills as he braced for another wave, gripping the crossbeam with all of his might. *BLAM*—the wave struck and howled across the ship as she rolled through its wake.

Edwin's feet went first, then the knife dropped to the deck, then Edwin's left hand lost grip. He flailed, letting go with his right hand now too, just as the ship whipped her masts back to center. Edwin was completely airborne for what felt like forever, watching his outstretched hands reach wildly for the net getting further from his grasp. Within the quickest of moments, Sam swooped over and grabbed Edwin before he could fall, hooking his arm with Edwin's and flinging them both against the net right below the swaying broken crossbeam. Edwin clung to the net just in time, scared shitless and pale. "She almost got you that time!" Sam yelled with a smirk.

"Almost!" Edwin yelled back, thankful to be attached but too distracted to hear the warning bell going off again. *BLAM*—another wave wreaked havoc across the ship. The broken beam swirled within the gust and clobbered Sam with a punching crack. His grasp broke away and Edwin watched him fall eighty feet to the main deck below. The crack of his skull was louder than the continuing warning bell. The next wave hit with another soaking punch that swept Sam's limp and broken body harshly across the deck.

Edwin held on while the two other AB, upon seeing Sam fall, burst into action and climbed up to cut the broken mount free. The topsail finally untangled, falling to the deck like a soaked, war-torn battle flag. Edwin was in shock, but there was no time to mourn. He was still clinging to the top end of a ship's mast in the middle of a storm. He and the other AB descended the netting, and he'd never been more thankful to be back on level footing. In this case, however, that level footing was slippery with the blood of his fallen friend and mentor.

For the next twenty minutes, the ship rolled and tossed about before finally breaking free of the storm's path and entering calm waters. Staggered crew, all bruised and cut from the turbulence, slowly caught their breath and secured the deck. Renault and the mates stood over the busted sail near the waist of the quarterdeck. Edwin and the other crew gathered around now too. "Pull it," Renault said to the closest AB. They yanked the sail back to reveal Sam's blood-leaking body lying in a grotesque contortion, with his skull cracked open and empty. Many of the AB grimaced, but many others simply sneered stoically, not un-used to seeing this sort of thing.

That's all that's left of the man who just saved my life, Edwin thought, staring off with remorse at one particular piece of brain matter sliding around the wet deck. Within the hour, Sam's body was wrapped in cloth and tossed out to sea rather unceremoniously. It went down as just another accident. No one had seen exactly what transpired when Sam fell, but Edwin internalized the truth of it as being his fault. Edwin and a few other AB were tasked with mopping up the blood and brains left behind. One of the AB found Edwin's knife off in a corner and returned it with a look like, *I've been there.* Edwin was rattled by Sam's death but remained steadfast.

Once off duty, Edwin lit a cigarette and reflected on how Sam had taught him to pre-roll smokes below deck before a shift, how that had become Edwin's daily morning ritual from then on. Which reminded Edwin of something else he used to do first thing every day—drink some goddamn coffee. He poked his head into the galley and found CK in a huff, trying to put the cook station back together after the beating it took from the storm. "Any luck with that coffee, by chance?" Edwin asked with trepidation.

"Luck? You motherfucker…I'm wearing your luck right here!" CK said, turning with a snarl to reveal an apron full of spilled coffee and spices.

"Of course," Edwin quipped.

"Oh yeah, take this hobo shit too. You fucking mook," CK said, handing over the percolator, now dented and destroyed. Edwin sulked and tossed it into a nearby rubbish bin on his way out. It was going to be a while before he got a decent cup of coffee.

5

VALPARAISO

The weeks dissolved into months. Calm seas blended with raging swells and the long days of tenuous labor smeared into foggy nights full of drinking regret away. Edwin had established cordialness with most bunkmates and had become quite good at playing poker between shifts. While on duty, though, Edwin was committed to the work. After two months, he was promoted from an Ordinary Seaman to an Able Bodied seaman, working directly under Kersey's management. Edwin thrived as an AB, continuing to use the tasks as a needed distraction from his constantly wandering mind. It was long hours of thankless and often backbreaking work, but Edwin had found serenity amongst it. The Salty Mariner encountered more storms over her course but weathered them all. Edwin was climbing masts and repairing busted sails on a regular basis, getting better and more agile with each outing. It became just as customary as hopping up the ladder to fix the shop's banner back home had been. Edwin was the first to volunteer every time, his way of silently reconciling for Sam's death.

Working on the ship released the anxiety Edwin felt in his chest and lower back. Love and loss and the debt and responsibility of running the shop back home were all problems getting further and further away. Now, all he had to do was take orders, and his duties on the ship had developed into a sort of routine that Edwin found comfort in. He was able to fall asleep at night with relative ease, knowing he had earned a restful slumber from a day's honest work. Work that Edwin did well, too, which didn't go unnoticed.

Maybe this is my calling, he thought, debating on whether to jump ship in San Francisco or stay onboard to make a career out of being a sailor. But he couldn't wind up back in Boston at the end of the Salty Mariner's run—not after Strickland and the fire. He pondered enlisting with a different ship in San Francisco, perhaps one going abroad, where Edwin would get to see the world as Lillian had. But then he'd have to rebuild bonds with a new crew and earn respect all over again. Edwin was lost in swirling thoughts, ultimately embracing the freedom of taking things as they came, even if only as a justification for not deciding.

Edwin and Kersey remained friendly and met up a few nights per week for a main deck drink. Kersey's mentorship was credited for Edwin's adherence to the job, which bode well for both of them with Renault and the mates crew. Even Mathews and Banyan had taken a liking to, and relied on, Edwin's solid work ethic. Edwin played along too, all the while keeping an eye on the both of them, aiming to strike when the opportunity for getting Lillian's harmonica back arose. Banyan had been playing it every once in a while, sneaking practice alone at night similar to how Edwin continued drawing in his copy of *The Mysterious Key*. Edwin pondered revenge while sketching abstract mise-en-scenes and caricatured crew portraits. He only showed his work to Kersey, who had become quite a fan, even pressuring Edwin to do a portrait of him one day—not knowing Edwin had already done so.

It was a late afternoon in April of 1873 when the Salty Mariner approached Valparaiso Bay on the southwest leg of Chile, nearly four months after leaving Boston. Valparaiso was a colorfully stoic city built between the ocean shore and green rolling hills, thriving wildly as the main go-between for ships sailing from one American coast to the other. At about half the distance to San Francisco, it would be the only resupply along the way and was a welcome sight to the crew. Just in time, too, as the grub and booze offerings on board had become quite paltry. Breakfast, lunch, and dinner had been broth and onion soup for the last three days. Edwin was ready to pillage and murder for a piece of fruit and a decent cup of coffee if he had to. The Salty Mariner eased into a slip and AB on duty anchored her up tight. Renault stood tall over the cockpit puffing on his pipe, as if the entire world would be waiting to greet his triumphant arrival.

Edwin had packed on ten pounds of muscle and ten times that in grit. His skin was tanned from the sun, his hair was longer and slicked back, and his proud mustache was now an even prouder goatee. He had earned thirty dollars playing poker over the last couple of months, which brought his total take up to one hundred and twenty. He stuffed fifty dollars in his boot, twenty dollars in his billfold, and left the rest within the pages of *The Mysterious Key* under his bunk.

Some crew were dismissed for leave once anchored, while others were assigned supply run and maintenance duties, then would join the rest of the men on leave until 10 p.m. the following evening for a midnight departure. Edwin was in the group picked for a galley supply run. He grabbed his coat and hat, then met up with Kersey to get a procurement list from CK. The rest of the resupply unit consisted of fellow AB Manning and Lucas, standing at the ready on the pier with rolling carts, and Banyan, waiting nearby with his arms crossed, acting pissed that he wasn't on leave. *What a horse's ass*, Edwin thought as he and Kersey approached.

"Come on, ya whifflers. Let's get this over with," Banyan said, taking the list from Kersey with a grunt.

The five of them sauntered up the dock toward a sprawled out and lively port market. Rows of gas lantern streetlights accented their path and made the bright colors of the buildings on Serrano Street pop even after sunset. Vendors and shopkeepers waved their arms and hollered for attention to their offerings as the Salty Mariner crew perused the aisles. They filled the two rolling carts with canned goods, meat and fish, fruit, booze, water, and hardware. It took them several runs and over three hours to get everything due on the list back to the ship.

After, Edwin and Kersey stood on the pier smoking cigarettes, with the Salty Mariner gently swaying behind them. Manning and Lucas strolled by with a casual wave, carrying their duffle bags. "Those two are jumping off," Kersey said.

"How can you tell?"

"No one brings their packs on leave 'less they ain't planning on coming back."

"Happens often, does it?"

"Damn near every time we dock."

"So we'll be short on labor for the rest of the go?"

"Nah, one way or another, we'll get replacements," Kersey boasted. "Always some fellas in a port city to hire or crimp. Cap isn't picky, so long as their backs are strong and they ain't too drunk. How the fuck ya think you got hired?"

"Blind fucking luck and pity, by my count," Edwin joked back. "Care to get some proper liquor and a real meal, or what have you planned for leave?"

"No offense, but I need a hot bath and the touch of a woman," Kersey said. "There's a brothel off Echaurren Square ya can get both 'bout a quarter mile from here if ya wanna follow. Two bits will get ya some fun, but a fiver will get ya the whole night."

"Tempting…" Edwin said, not sure if he was ready to be with another woman and pay for the affection. Across the way, Banyan disembarked the ship sporting his finest coat and slacks, which were still shit, but by his standards was dressed up for a night out, hurrying along as if already late.

"Wobbly sack of fuck…" Kersey said, just loud enough for Edwin to hear.

"I've taken shits with more backbone," Edwin bantered along.

"The fuck you two under scrubs gawking at?" Banyan barked as he passed by on his way to town. Edwin and Kersey waved him off, laughing to themselves as they finished their smokes and strolled toward town as well.

"Think I'll track down a steak and some bourbon. Shall we rendezvous midday tomorrow?" Edwin asked, keeping an eye on Banyan's path.

"Sure thing," Kersey said. "You just think of me plowing some sweet-looking zook while ya chomp on that steak, beefer. Have a good night," he added with a smirk. Edwin saluted Kersey sarcastically as they split ways—Kersey toward Mid Town, and Edwin toward wherever the hell Banyan was going.

The streets were vibrant with activity. Edwin kept his distance as he tailed Banyan through busy corridors of cafes, pubs, and street vendors. Wafts of spicy cooked meat, lantern oil smoke, and exotic perfumes penetrated the air. A mix of pasty English and American sailors mingled with sun-kissed locals that all seemed to be having the time of their lives.

Edwin followed Banyan into a saloon signed "Casa De Chao," built from adobe and imported Oregon pine wood. A zamacueca band serenaded the eclectic crowd overflowing from the streets, and there wasn't a sober individual in sight. Banyan met up with Mathews and a couple of Chilean women sitting at a table in the corner. Edwin blended in at the bar, taking a seat with his hat brim drawn low, not actually knowing why he had followed Banyan here but going with it all the same. Edwin ordered bourbon and steak from the vest-clad and mustached bartender, glancing over at Banyan and

Mathews drinking tequila and scarfing empanadas like gluttonous pigs.

Edwin scanned the room while waiting for his food to arrive. Locals mixed with travelers dancing and laughing in the center of the saloon, while quieter men sat in booths along the walls, getting hammered or staring off longingly. Edwin was three drinks deep when a beautiful dark-skinned waitress in a bright flowing dress dropped off a plate of bloody steak and potatoes. Edwin dug in with vigor, savoring the first few bites before shoveling the rest of it quickly into his mouth. He had a decent buzz going, and could tell Mathews and Banyan did as well. They were getting dumb and loud in the corner, becoming more aggressive with their dates—local prostitutes, by Edwin's count, based on them actually putting up with Mathews and Banyan's sloppy behavior.

Edwin gnawed on the steak bone for scraps and debated his next move. He could follow Banyan around all night and still not get a proper moment to confront him about the harmonica. Plus, it had to be done in a way that wouldn't jeopardize his position on the Salty Mariner. It would be another three or four months before docking in San Francisco, and Edwin couldn't just jump ship in the middle of a foreign country. Although, for the slightest of moments, the thought of staying in Chile did spark excitement in Edwin's wandering mind. *That would show them*, he thought, whoever the *them* were.

Banyan was raring to leave now, putting his jacket on and signaling the prostitutes to do the same. Mathews, however, had imbibed a bit too much while waiting for Banyan to arrive and was slumped over in the corner of the booth, bobbing his head and passing out. Banyan tried waking him up with a few swats on the face, to no avail, then quickly gave in to making the best of having both prostitutes, whose fees were paid in advance and split equally, all to himself instead. Edwin settled his bill at the bar, still trying to figure out his next move. Perhaps he'd follow Banyan and the women to what Edwin assumed would just be an alley to fuck in, by the way Banyan was chomping at the bits—but then what? Mug him mid-fuck? Wait until he was done fucking…then mug him? This was unfamiliar territory to Edwin. *I should just give it a rest*, he thought. *Wait until a better opportunity presents itself.*

Edwin surveyed the room once more, noticing some local farmers sitting at a booth nearby, wearing tattered ponchos and black straw hats. Their worn faces read to Edwin as a sign that these men had a strong work ethic for hire. "Do any of you speak English?" Edwin asked, approaching with a friendly grin. The hombre he asked shook his head and pointed to another farmer sitting a few chairs away, with an even rougher-looking face and a scar across his cheek. "Do you speak English?" Edwin asked.

"Si," the farmer replied with a slight slur.

"Does that mean yes?"

"Si," the farmer said, grinning wider.

"How would you and your friends like to make twenty dollars?" Edwin asked, holding up cash from his billfold while checking over his shoulders.

The farmer nodded, adjusting his hat to see better. "Para que...For what?"

Edwin took a seat and leaned in close. "See the man there with the derby hat?" Edwin pointed out Banyan as he stood to leave with the prostitutes.

"Si," the farmer said. "Looks like he having a good night...Bueno."

"Not if I can help it," Edwin said. "He stole something from me. A harmonica."

"Harmonica?" the farmer asked, putting his hands to his mouth like he was playing one. "Instrumento?"

"Si. Instrumento," Edwin replied, getting anxious.

"Why no you ask him yourself?"

"It's complicated. He can't know I instigated it."

"In-sti-gat-ed?" the farmer asked with a twisted expression.

"I need someone else to do it for me. That's the job," Edwin said. "And it has to be tonight. Right now. You can keep his billfold, I just want the instrumento."

The farmer smiled. "We take?"

"Yes. You take and give to me. Deal?"

The farmer leaned over to the two men sitting next to him and laid it all out in Spanish. They all nodded in agreement. "Bueno, jefe. We'll do it," the farmer said. "Pagar antes…You pay now."

Edwin shook his head. "Half now. The rest after."

The farmer wrinkled his face. "Trato justo," he said, smirking approval. Edwin handed half the money to the farmer and they shook hands. Banyan made his way out with the prostitutes, leaving Mathews slumped over in the booth. The farmer and his hombres finished their drinks and tracked Banyan. Edwin took a deep breath, following them out as they followed Banyan, keeping his distance.

It was well past midnight, yet the streets were still buzzing with booze-induced ruckus. Banyan drunkenly led his employed female companions toward a modest hotel a few blocks over. Edwin lit a cigarette and observed from across the street as his employed bandito-pushes gained on Banyan. One of the hombres ran up ahead from across the street, and then got into position near a dark alley between buildings. The other hombre and the farmer closed in from behind. Banyan stumbled closer to the alley with the ladies in tow. The first hombre took a step in front of them with his arms crossed, blocking the way. "Kick rocks," Banyan slurred, waving him off.

"Blanco!" the farmer said from behind, getting Banyan to turn around—*CRACK*—the farmer swung a bottle over Banyan's head and pushed him into the alley. The prostitutes winced and went to scream, but the two hombres covered their mouths and ushered them into the shadows of the alley behind Banyan. Edwin tensed up, wondering if this had all gone too far. He threw out his cigarette and ran across the street. In the alley, the farmer and his hombres had Banyan backed up to the wall. They let the prostitutes run off and pulled knives out.

"You fuckers…" Banyan slurred. "You gonna mug me <u>and</u> scatter my women?! Better stick me then too, 'cuz I'm'a kill ya for this!"

"Give us your billfold and the 'monica!" the farmer ordered.

"The fucking what?" Banyan quipped, sincerely confused.

"Monica! Instrumento! Give it now!" the farmer barked.

"Fuck ya, spic-O!" Banyan sneered, reaching behind his hip for a revolver, but the hombres were faster. One threw a punch to Banyan's jaw while the other stabbed him in the stomach, twisting the blade across his abdomen. Banyan dropped the revolver without getting a shot off and collapsed to his knees, gripping at his bleeding gut. Edwin grimaced from his vantage point around the corner. The two hombres held Banyan up by his arms while the farmer riffled through his pockets, coming up with a decently stuffed billfold, the revolver, and the crumpled up Salty Mariner supply run list from earlier. Banyan balled up on the cold concrete when they dropped him, bleeding out and moaning as the hombres took inventory of his wallet. Edwin ran up in a panic, more concerned now with getting the harmonica back then blowing his cover with Banyan. The farmer shrugged and held up the stash for Edwin to see.

"No 'monica, jefe," the farmer said.

"You searched him?" Edwin asked in a huff.

"Si."

"Fucking hell," Edwin said, shaking his head. "Just go…"

The farmer wrinkled his face. "You pay," he said as a threat.

"Take the billfold and pistol. You weren't supposed to hurt him."

"Mierda...shit happens," the farmer said with a smirking shrug. "You pay or we take, blanco." The two hombres stepped closer with their knives.

"Fine," Edwin huffed, handing over another ten dollars with a snarl. The farmer took it with Banyan's stash and motioned for the hombres to follow him out of the alley.

"Mala suerte," the farmer said as they left. "Better luck next time."

Edwin growled and stewed. He still didn't have the harmonica, and now his boss was tamped up and bleeding out in an alley at his feet, despite it all.

"Morris...how did...why the hell..." Banyan murmured from the ground between spits of blood and agony. "You fucking lump...you did this to me?"

Edwin took a knee and pulled Banyan up by his shirt collar. "You did this to yourself. Now where's my fucking harmonica?" he asked with urgency.

"What the hell you talkin' 'bout?" Banyan said, still desperately confused.

"Where is it, Banyan?" Edwin said, getting more aggressive. "My dead wife gave that to me! You thieving fucking inbreed!"

Banyan reeled in pain, realizing now who Edwin was but still more concerned about tucking his guts back into his split-open belly. "I ain't got it...just help me..." he muttered.

"I'll help ya, alright..." Edwin snarled, then pulled Banyan's collar tight around his neck and choked it up against his throat. He held Banyan down until he finally went limp and keeled over. Edwin stood slowly, trembling and snapping out of a blind rage. *This has definitely gone too far*, he thought. *Now what*?

He exited the shadows of the alley in a hurry, keeping his hat low while making tracks through the crowd. He kept rubbing his face, trying to sober up, replaying Banyan's death rattle in his mind. *Tighten it up*, he thought, sick to his stomach and angry for losing control of his impulses. All the while, he was equally enthralled by the rush of mischievous adrenaline pulsing through his veins knowing that Banyan was stuck and rotting in an alley, where he belonged.

Now it was just a matter of getting away with it, but *where the fuck was the harmonica?* Edwin arrived at the port, marching up to the Salty Mariner and the AB on guard duty sitting on a dock rail reading a newspaper. "Rough night, Morris?" said the mean middle-aged mutt named Murphy.

"Nothing I can't handle," Edwin replied, questioning said statement internally.

"Good on ya," Murphy said like he gave a shit, waving off with a sloppy grin.

"We'll see..." Edwin muttered as he passed by and went up the ramp to the main deck of the ship. Robinson was drunk asleep by the gangway next to an empty bottle and a rifle, but the deck was otherwise vacant. Edwin snuck down to the mates' quarters and went for what he deemed to be Banyan's bunk. Edwin dug through a duffle bag, a small nightstand, and then lifted the bedroll—there it was. Edwin clutched Lillian's harmonica against his chest, vowing to never let it out of his sight again.

6

GETTING AWAY WITH IT

"Come, come, no tricks, boy. What ... leaving the house at this hour and in such ..."

"Why, Hester ..." He took the grip ... looked ...

"Yes, and well you ... the bolts would have been ... by this time ... upon me, I'd leave it ... and play ghost ...

"Leave my boy ... in daylight; this ... two ... in our fashion ..."

She told him ... in her arms, and ... afraid ... While ... finished he was ... and, looking half way down ... had ... dark, you alone have ... go out. I walk in ... Hester that's the truth ... won't ... you see, and I'm sorry for it. Don't be bundled ... in self ... for come this way ... I just ... up ... crawl back to bed ... and I entreat you ...

"Just a trifle ... nothing. Poor lad ... to follow or he looks ... it's dangerous to go ... this way," said Hester ... "my self ...

"It won't last, ... the ... more than ... sound. Don't tell me ... please, else ... If ... that's not pleasant ... and ... your knowledge ... like a mother, and ... that you feel ... with all my ...

He held out his arm with the look of a ... Hester. Remember ... time ... and he was a mother ... stroked the curly ... of his forehead and kiss ... thought ... her own ... down at her head.

"Good night, dear," ... saying much. I ... that will ensure you ... rest hereafter ...

With that she ... but would have ... she may, on the ... ... of ... inherit ... possession of human ... ... for he laughed ... his cheeks.

Edwin stuffed the harmonica in his pocket, then froze in panicked thought. He'd need to make it look like Banyan had abandoned his post to abscond from suspicion, or he himself would need to jump ship and avoid the aftermath all together. Which meant no transport to San Francisco, or at least not any time soon, and not on the Salty Mariner. *Hell no*, he thought, then quickly bundled all of Banyan's slop into a duffle bag from under the bunk, tossing it over his shoulder and snaking his way out of the mates' quarters to the main deck. While passing the captain's quarters, the sound of laughter and moaning from within caught his attention. Curiosity got the best of Edwin, as it usually did, and he snuck closer to investigate.

The door was ajar just enough to see inside. Outlined by the smoky glow of a lantern, Renault was entertaining three Chilean women—all naked and drunk, cavorting into each other on the bed. Renault had only his hat on, gripping a bottle of brandy as he took one woman from behind while she was pleasuring another laid out in front of them, who had the third woman sitting on her face. *Son of a bitch,* Edwin thought. *Good for that old fucker.* Edwin was not used to, and was intrigued by, the sight of such debauchery. Torn between continuing to watch and knowing that getting caught doing so would be the least of his worries if it were while ransacking Banyan's belongings to cover up his murder, Edwin eventually refocused on the mission at hand and snuck down the hallway.

With the duffle bag in tow, Edwin reached the main deck and peeked over the port side rail. Murphy was still on guard, bitterly smoking while thinking about how much fun the others must be having on leave. Edwin pivoted across the waist of the ship and reached the starboard rail. "Good riddance you fuck," he muttered as he tossed Banyan's belongings overboard. A small splash rippled below in the dark.

"What the hell ya doing, Morris?" Robinson slurred, looming nearby.

Edwin turned, trying to control his shock and gauging whether or not Robinson had seen him ditch the bag. "Too much liquor, I reckon—puking my fucking guts out," he said, playing up a sick stomach. Robinson's stone-faced glare gave nothing away. Edwin assumed the worst, thinking he was about to be called out for murder and hung by his neck to atone for it.

"Ay," Robinson slurred. "Should'a seen me on my first leave. Must'a drank all the rum in port. Was fuckin' chunking for days."

Edwin nodded, relieved that his charade seemed to be working. "Quite a city," he said to keep it going. "I've never seen anything like it."

"That's one way to put it," Robinson said bitterly, then offered Edwin a pull from the rum he was drinking on. Edwin took the bottle and gulped a hearty sip.

"Where are you from, Robinson?" Edwin asked. Robinson, suddenly bored with the conversation he had inadvertently started, raised the bottle, nodded smugly, and left without a further word, sauntering over to the quarterdeck to drink alone in peace. Edwin stood by the rail, taking in the calm sea with a deep sigh of relief. He reached into his pocket and felt the harmonica in his hands, its sentimentality feeling so much heavier than its actual weight. Edwin desperately wanted to play it but knew he couldn't for fear of raising suspicion. He placed it back in his pocket and retired to his bunk below deck. He was the only sailor that spent the one night he didn't have to sleep onboard sleeping onboard.

The next morning, Edwin woke from a night of bad dreams, relieved to be in one piece within the safety of a lumpy bunk. He rolled three cigarettes and made his way to the galley for breakfast, only to find it dark and vacated. CK and the rest of the AB were taking full advantage of their leave and would be damned to spend it onboard the ship as Edwin had.

Robinson was asleep near some crates on the main deck, while Murphy slept on the dock using newssheets as a blanket. Edwin disturbed neither as he marched on in search of coffee and a hot breakfast.

The brightly colored seaside architecture of the city was even more vibrant under the morning light. The pastel blues, greens, and yellows gave the busy hilly streets an extra pop of liveliness. Edwin found a public eatery with outdoor seating, ordering fried ham and eggs with two coffees straight away. He watched the steady market crowd bustle with life all around him as he ate. Fishmongers and flower girls kicked around with con artists and bread makers, all intersecting within a never-ending herd of commerce.

Over a third and fourth cup of coffee, Edwin pondered which one of them was going to find Banyan rotting in the street and kick up a fit about it. Any minute now, Edwin expected to hear screams and emergency bells. When a local church tower chimed at noon, Edwin was sure it was the impending doom he was bracing for, but the screams and alarms never came. Edwin sat there for hours watching the day pass him by. He eventually ordered lunch and his coffee refills became ale refills. The church bell chimed six times now and Edwin figured he'd had enough. His shift started at 10 p.m., and the Salty Mariner's departure to San Francisco was set for midnight. Edwin settled the bill and made tracks back to port, stopping at the market along the way to resupply on whiskey and tobacco.

The sun was setting colorfully over the ocean when Edwin paced down the dock toward the Salty Mariner's slip. His steps were cautious, imagining that somehow Banyan had survived and would be waiting on the main deck with local police to haul him away in shackles. But no such operation was found as Edwin made his way up the ramp. AB prepped workstations while Renault and Robinson consulted maps near the stern. No one was hunting for Edwin or really even gave a shit that he had come aboard. *You're getting away with it*, he thought, *just a few more hours.*

"Morris!" Kersey yelled from the gangway. "What in the hell happened?"

This is it, Edwin thought, *I'm fucked...* "Good morning," he said timidly.

"It's night, you wet-head," Kersey joked. "Where the fuck you yonder to? Said we'd meet up midday, and you never showed, ya fuckin' yegg."

"Ah, right...It slipped my mind," Edwin said with relief.

"Yeah, figures. Well, you should'a seen the bazoo on this angel I greased with last night, my friend, she was as hot as a lit stick of dynamite," Kersey said, shaking his head with a laugh, then went on to tell Edwin all about his sexual exploits. They bantered along the quarterdeck over Spanish brandy Kersey had scored in town. Edwin told Kersey that all he'd done on leave was eat, drink, and sleep. Kersey had no suspicions, and it appeared that neither did anyone else onboard when 10 p.m. came about and signaled the beginning of their shift. Edwin tightened his boots and fell in line loading supplies into the cargo hold. Renault smoked his pipe, overseeing from the dock while Robinson reviewed the manifest, checking his pocket watch with concern.

"Where the fuck are Mathews and Banyan?" Robinson snarled. "Anyone see them on leave?" None of the AB on duty had, shaking their heads and remaining focused on their tasks. Edwin shrugged the question off in suit; of course he hadn't seen Mathews or killed Banyan the night before. He knew Banyan was toast, but what the hell had happened to Mathews? Probably collecting Banyan's body for evidence, and would at any moment be here leading the authorities on a raid to thwart Edwin's escape, or so Edwin let himself continue to think in paranoia. "Fucking mopers are late again," Robinson said, glaring and tapping his watch.

"What's the count?" Renault asked, joining Robinson by the dock rail.

"Down two AB plus Mathews and Banyan," Robinson reported.

"Round up some fresh meat," Renault replied with a sneer. "We push at midnight."

"Ay," Robinson said, then turned toward the ship and yelled for Kersey.

Kersey secured a crate latch and approached Robinson for his orders.

"We're down a few heads. Fetch us a crimp in town. Take someone with ya in case 'dem dead dicks need to be carted. Get on it with haste!" Robinson barked.

"Ay," Kersey replied. "Morris! You're with me."

Edwin tied off a rope and met up with Kersey in front of Robinson and Renault. Renault eyeballed Edwin like he could see right through him, or so Edwin felt from the glare. Robinson handed petty cash from a purchase folio over to Kersey. "We need four men. Here's five hundred, but try to get them for a hundred or less per head, got it?" Robinson said.

"Crystal clear, sir, hundred a head," Kersey said.

"Or less. Go," Robinson barked.

"We're on it," Kersey said, leading Edwin off the ship and up the dock.

"The hell we doing?" Edwin asked when they got out of earshot from the others.

"We 'bout to fetch us some new recruits. They don't always just show up knocking for a job after bedding the owner's daughter," Kersey said with a playful jab at Edwin.

"You know where to go?" Edwin asked.

"Yeah, man," Kersey said. "They call 'em rizadors 'round here. Some real bad-apple hombres that help secure AB for waiting ships."

Edwin still didn't quite understand but was happy to be talking about anything besides his own crime spree, nonetheless. "Robinson mentioned fetching a crimp?"

"Just follow me and keep your mouth jammed," Kersey said, leading Edwin through the busy nightlife of Echaurren Square, ducking behind street vendors as they reached an ocean-facing alley that descended along a back row of trading houses. A tall, mean-looking black hat- and vest-clad doorman sat under a lantern smoking a joint, guarding the entrance to the basement of one of the buildings. The doorman stiffened his posture and snarled as they approached. Edwin wondered if they were in the right place as Kersey stepped up with a friendly wave. "Amigo…donde rizador?"

The doorman stared Kersey and Edwin down, taking a steady rip from his joint and letting out a thick puff of smoke. It didn't smell like any tobacco Edwin was familiar with, but the skunky pine aroma was both repulsive and enticing. "Un momento," the doorman said, then disappeared into a dark hallway.

Edwin leaned in to ask a question, but Kersey cut him off with a raised finger like, *Not now*. The doorman returned from darkness, motioning for Kersey and Edwin to enter. Edwin didn't want to but followed Kersey in, ready for anything. When the door slammed shut behind them, he shuddered like an idiot. "Calm those nerves, Morris," Kersey said just above a whisper. "Makes us look like amateurs," he added with a snaky grin.

The doorman chuckled as well, then offered his joint to Edwin. "Calmese...easy," he said with a laid-back smile.

Edwin raised an eyebrow and debated taking the joint. "Tobacco?" he asked.

"Y hierba," the doorman replied.

"Tobacco mixed with cannabis. Rattles you up, in a good way," Kersey jumped in to explain, then reached out for the joint and took a rip of it himself before handing it to Edwin. Edwin took a steady hit, then handed it back to the doorman.

"Gracias," Kersey said.

"Gracias," Edwin said, echoing Kersey's lead. The doorman nodded slyly then ushered them further into the basement. At the end of the dark hallway was a cavernous holding area with a row of crude-looking jail cells. Two more crimps and their boss sat at a table in the middle of the room, playing cards and drinking. The boss, Montero, was a stout and scarred man with tall riding boots, a black cowboy hat, and a leather poncho that sat more like a cape. Kersey nodded with a slight bow. Two disheveled Englishmen were passed out but looked dead in the cells nearby. They were in their underwear, covered in dirt, and clutching jars of moonshine.

"You have not been here before," Montero said with a thick Chilean accent, pointing to Edwin. "You have," he continued, pointing to Kersey.

"Yes, last winter, I believe it was. You helped us fetch marineros back then, and we lookin' for the same deal tonight," Kersey explained. "This is Morris, he's an AB with me on the Salty Mariner." Edwin stood still, wondering how he'd ended up in a black-market labor camp and coming to terms with whatever the hell was in that cigarette he'd just smoked.

"Si…Bueno…I have two able-bodied marineros at the moment," Montero said. "My men are scouring the streets for more, if you can wait until morning."

"Pushing off in an hour. If two's what ya got, two is what we'll take," Kersey said, then fished out one hundred dollars of the petty cash. "Fifty a piece?" Kersey asked.

"One hundred fifty each. They are trained and sturdy," Montero countered.

Kersey held up another hundred-dollar bill. "One hundred each."

Montero smirked evilly. "Maybe two hundred each and I don't cut you," he snarled.

This shit-kicker can negotiate, Edwin thought. *Damn, I'm parched*.

Kersey shrugged, pulling out an additional hundred dollars. "One fifty a piece it is."

"Gran oferta, bien," Montero said with a grin, then whistled for his men to fetch the jailed Englishmen. Kersey placed three hundred dollars on the table while Edwin wondered if anyone else was getting lightheaded. One of Montero's men held open the cell door while the other splashed a bucket of water across the Englishmen. They stirred and kicked but were still mostly passed out.

"We'll take 'em like that and they can sleep it off on the ship," Kersey said, not fazed at all by what was happening. "Got a cart we can borrow?"

Montero barked more orders in Spanish, then stuffed the money into his pocket. "My men will meet you outside. Adios."

Ten minutes later, Kersey and Edwin were pushing a rickety cart containing the two Englishmen, dressed but still passed out, through the outskirts of Echaurren Square, making no effort to hide their human cargo. "What the hell just happened?" Edwin asked, stunted.

"What do you mean?"

"Who were those men? Who the hell are these men?"

"Local crimps," Kersey replied. "Mopes here prolly ran a tab they couldn't pay, so them crimps buy 'em out to bounty off to folks needing labor such as ourselves. It's pretty simple."

"And we expect them to just fall in line when they sober up on the deck of a ship?"

"I'm sure they know the drill. Blowing ya wad on credit in a port city is a one-way ticket outta town. Even dumb-dumbs know that. It really ain't that bad a deal, though, if ya embrace it. They'll work off the debt, then catch a return gig back, or not. 'Dey just like ol' Salty, going with whichever way the wind blows 'em," Kersey said to sum it up.

"You make it sound so straightforward," Edwin said.

"Ain't it, though? Besides, fuck 'em...not my kin," Kersey said, smirking. "They get a ride and we make our crew quota. End of the bottle."

Edwin cracked a laugh, unsure if it was Kersey's carefree regard or a goofy response to the cannabis. "What's the law think about all this?"

Kersey smirked. "Stress not, Morris. Crimping ain't even illegal in the states."

"Well, when we get arrested, I'll tell the buzzers you say so."

"Didn't that hombre's spliff calm you out yet?" Kersey joked. "Relax."

"Feeling quite relaxed, now that you mention it."

"Good, go with that. May be the last time for a while."

Edwin shrugged with a grin and did as he was told. They pushed the cart across the crowded streets of the market toward the pier, and indeed, no one seemed to care about the two foreign sailors carting passed-out wet-heads off to sea. The last twenty-four hours in Chile had become an epiphany-sized indication to Edwin of how little he actually knew about this new line of work he'd found himself in. And to a greater degree, how little he really knew about *anything* outside of Boston. His perception of the size of the world around him was ever expanding, giving Edwin hope and making him feel even smaller all at once. With luck, just maybe he could hide between the cracks.

Kersey had been talking the whole time they'd been plodding along, but Edwin was lost in his thoughts, realizing it only when Kersey asked, "Know what I mean?" for a second time.

Not a clue, Edwin thought with a shrug. "Definitely," he said.

They made their way back to the Salty Mariner by a quarter to midnight. AB helped them stow the new recruits onboard to sleep it off, leaving the cart behind on the dock for Montero's men to pick up later. Robinson loomed over with his pocket watch. "Only two?" he snarled.

"All they had unless we wait until morning," Kersey said.

"We push in ten minutes," Renault announced from behind the wheel.

"Ay, captain," Robinson said to Renault. "How much?" he asked Kersey.

"Three hundred on short notice. Crimp said they're ship ready."

"That's a shit price," Robinson said.

"You're welcome," Kersey replied with bite. Robinson turned away, barking orders at crew readying the ship for departure. Renault stepped over to peruse the new recruits.

"They look like a couple of cake-eaters," Renault said. "Just more labor for you AB, if they're shit." Renault paced, then squared up directly with Edwin. "Enjoy your leave, Morris?" he asked with a stern demeanor.

Ah hell, Edwin thought, *he knows*. "Yes, sir," he stated nervously as Renault glared. Edwin bit his tongue, waiting for Renault to expose him for the peeping, thieving, murdering fraud fuck that he was.

"Anchors away!" Renault yelled through Edwin to the rest of the crew. Edwin gulped and nodded. Renault returned to his post.

"What the fuck just happened?" Kersey said, amused and confused.

"I'm not sure," Edwin said. "But I think that cannabis has kicked in." The Salty Mariner crew got to work preparing to set sail. Edwin fell in to his tasks and it seemed that, although embarrassed, Edwin was going to make it out of Valparaiso without being caught for his crimes. He took a deep breath and shifted his focus whole-heartedly to the work at hand.

"It's Mathews!" one of the AB yelled, pointing to the dock. Edwin snapped his gaze to look with the rest of the crew. Mathews stumbled down the pier barefoot with a look of rage and exhaustion. His clothes were dirty and unkempt, and he held a bloody cold-water-soaked bandage over his head nursing a wound, spitting-mad as he approached the ship.

"Where the fuck ya been?" Robinson barked, looming over the cockpit rail.

"I hate this place!" Mathews snarled. "Every fucking time!" He huffed and cussed and labored up the ramp, just as AB were preparing to stow it. Most crew kept to their tasks, but Edwin moseyed closer to hear what was being said.

"Banyan fixing to show up too?" Robinson asked, meeting Mathews on the deck.

"That weasel ain't here?" Mathews asked with shock and anger. "I got a few choice words for his zook-thieving mug, that's for fucking sure!"

"He is absent and presumed a jumper," Robinson said. "So were you."

"I ain't no jumper! Banyan ditched me drunk and swooped my Mary. I woke up beat to hell and robbed in the town clown's drunk tank. Had to barter my fucking boots for bail!"

"You want slack for not handling your liquor?" Robison barked. "All that shit story means to me and my manifest is that yer late for duty!" Robinson mean-mugged Mathews into submission. Mathews sunk his shoulders, struggling not to say something that he'd regret. Edwin pretended to be busy nearby, hoping his cover was still maintained. Mathews did what he was told, disappearing below deck. Edwin tied off the crate he was securing and moved on to the next as the Salty Mariner eased away from the docks of Valparaiso, en route to San Francisco.

I made it, Edwin thought. *Calm seas and easy winds from here.* He leaned back against the port side rail and took in a deep breath of the ocean breeze. The water was indeed calm, and the winds were pushing the ship off with a scoot, catching the Salty Mariner's proud sails and billowing them forward into the midnight-blue horizon. Edwin pulled a cigarette from his chest pocket and ducked below a rail to light it with a match, enjoying the view ahead of him...until *SMACK*— Mathews swiped his meaty knuckles and backhanded Edwin across the mouth, smashing the cigarette and sending Edwin down hard to the deck.

"You flim-flam!" Mathews hollered, launching a kick now. "What did you do?"

Edwin threw his hands up, pleading, "What's your fucking quarrel?"

"My quarrel?" Mathews said with fire in his eyes. "My fuckin' quarrel is you!"

SMACK—CRUNCH—Mathews launched a hard balled-up fist right into Edwin's nose, breaking bone and knocking Edwin out cold.

7

SAN FRANCISCO OR BUSTED

when he forgot himself, he kissed the small hand, saying
impulsively. "My dear Lillian, I want nothing but your
goodwill and your ——" here he caught his breath.

"You have that already, and I want something to
add to it. But ——" As she spoke she dropped a little locket which
had slipped ——— forward ———

He stooped to pick it up, and in doing so observed
and exclaimed, "Why, this is mamma's ———, sweetheart,
Paul. I beg your pardon, and, tell Hester that we had one
because you took no notice of them. Let me see, it is pretty."

"Very ———," answered the boy, without looking at the pictu—

"Do you like it so much?" ——— interesting ———
interested with ———

"Very ———," he played ———

"Would you be broken-hearted, as they say in the ———?" asked
the girl, melodramatically.

"Yes, Miss Lillian, or anyone who is older."

"Dear me, how very nice it is just to have anyone care for
one so much," said the girl ——— I wonder if anybody eve—
will for me."

Love comes ——————— late,
And maketh ———————
Forever ——— find us more ———
And ———————

said ——— of Hester ——— strayed from him, for his ———
——— the sweetheart of yours ———
——— with a curious yet wistful ———

——— if there was no 'perhaps' about ———
——— handling of the eye and the ———
——— he forgot the boy's reply.
——— My young ——— I must ——— anything ———
——— pains.

——— little lady, and ———
Paul ———

Edwin slowly emerged from the dark of unconsciousness. It was the next morning and a thick fog surrounded the Salty Mariner as she whisked north-northwest through the Pacific Ocean. Edwin's hands were bound with rope to the quarterdeck rail. His nose was surrounded by dry, crusted blood and he was soaking wet. Robinson stood nearby, having just thrown a bucket full of water at Edwin's face to wake him up. Surrounding Robinson, encircling the opposite side of the main deck, were Kersey, Foster, CK, and the whole mess of boatswain and AB. Mathews sat on a barrel a few feet away, while Renault paced in the middle of it all, holding court. Edwin curled up to the rail, trying to collect his bearings. "You stand accused, Mr. Morris," Renault announced with authority.

"Of what, exactly?" Edwin said, knowing it could be any number of things.

"That's what yer 'bout to tell us," Renault stated.

"Where the fuck is Banyan and what'd ya do to him?" Mathews hollered.

"The hell are you talking about?" Edwin barked, still trying to gauge how much anyone really knew about it. Before Edwin could finish a denial, though, Mathews held up the harmonica. Edwin's teeth trembled as he stared at it in Mathews' dirty mutt fingers. *Shit*, Edwin thought, *I might be fucking the rooster on this on…*

Mathews had become so overwhelmingly annoyed by Banyan's constant practice with the harmonica that he confiscated it nearly two months ago, then inadvertently became curious about playing it himself. It was Mathews, not Banyan, that had been sneaking practice with the harmonica in the dark of night that Edwin had heard all those times he was drawing on the other side of the deck. Edwin couldn't have predicted that these two meatheads were both so musically inclined, or that it was actually Mathews's bedroll the harmonica was stowed under when he cleared out all of what he thought to be Banyan's belongings the night before. When Mathews returned disheveled from leave, learned of Banyan's absence, and then found his own bunk pilfered, he knew something was afoul. Murphy and Robinson had both stated seeing Edwin poking around that night while most crew were on leave. Edwin instantly became Mathews's only suspect, accusing him first with the flat front of his meaty, swinging fist…

"So I figure Morris got to Banyan sometime after he abandoned me and stole my damn whore, then tried to cover it up by tossing out what he thought to be Banyan's bunk to make it look like he'd jumped ship," Mathews explained smugly to the crowd, then mean-mugged Edwin directly to say, "Except ya tossed my shit out instead. I had a hunch 'bout it, but after finding this spit-box on ya, I'm sure as hell that whatever happened to Banyan had something to do with you."

Edwin couldn't believe it—Mathews wasn't as dumb as he looked.

"Is any of that true?" Renault asked Edwin.

"Of course, it is!" Mathews insisted. "Only questions are whether or not Banyan is still alive, and where the fuck Morris left him to rot!"

AB muttered amongst themselves. Kersey stared at Edwin with disbelief. Renault raised his hand to calm the commotion. "Is what he says true or not, boy?" he asked Edwin.

Edwin weighed the options of his response. They must not have found Banyan's body if Mathews was still asking where he was, so all anyone seemed to know for sure was what Edwin had done onboard the ship. There might be a way out of this yet, if he kept his tongue sharp. "It's not *not* true," Edwin said.

"You sarcastic son of a bitch!" Mathews yelled, then stood and pulled out a blade.

"I want him to say it!" Renault barked to Mathews, turning a red-hot gaze to Edwin. "Speak now, or I'll let him at ya! Did you accost Banyan? Over a fucking harmonica?"

It did, indeed, sound insane when Edwin heard Renault ask him about it out loud. *Yes! It's true! Now go fuck your mother!* he thought, but Edwin was not inclined to confess so easily; they'd have to prove him guilty. "What Mathews said I did to his bunk is true," Edwin proclaimed, speaking only to the half-truths he was ready to admit to, pausing for a flutter of commotion from the crew. Renault silenced them all before Edwin continued his routine. "But I swear I don't know what happened to Banyan."

"Horse shit! You fucking misfeasor, you!" Mathews protested.

"Explain yourself!" Renault barked to Edwin. "Or is your only rebuttal to say that you're merely a thief and not a murderer?"

"I'm neither..." Edwin proclaimed, selling it as true.

"Then why thrash the bunk?" Renault asked like a dagger.

"Mathews and Banyan are the thieves, sir, I only wanted back what was mine." Edwin let that linger for a moment.

Mathews calked his head like, *What the hell is he talking about?* Edwin grit his teeth and went on, "Mathews and Banyan robbed me in Boston…stole almost a thousand dollars and that harmonica from me."

"What the fuck you saying?" Mathews grunted, stymied by the accusation as he realized Edwin was whom he and Banyan had, in fact, mugged on their leave in Boston.

"Is that true?" Renault barked at Mathews, who could only return a confused shrug. "Is that why you enlisted?" Renault blasted back to Edwin.

"No, sir. Didn't know it was them 'til I heard that harmonica being played onboard."

"You expect me to believe that, after realizing the grunts that robbed you were on board, you didn't seek revenge?" Renault asked Edwin. Mathews and the others leaned in, eager for Edwin's response.

"No, sir. Of course, I wanted to confront both them goddamn jackrollers, but I couldn't blow this employment opportunity. So, I waited. Took advantage of how vacant the ship was on leave and ransacked their bunks. Which is where I found *my property*, swiped it back, and tossed 'dey shit overboard out of spite," Edwin said with a passionate rage that almost made him believe it himself. "I got no idea why Banyan didn't show up or what he got up to on leave. What I'm damn sure of, though, is that Banyan and Mathews are a bunch of no-good-doers and reap what they sow. I wouldn't be surprised if it finally caught up to either of them rat-bastards."

Renault digested what Edwin said with curiosity, as did the rest of the crew. "Did you and Banyan rob this man while on leave in Boston?" Renault asked Mathews.

"It's not *not* true," Mathews said with his dumb look crinkling more like a scorned child than a hardened sailor accused of a crime. Edwin could feel Kersey and the rest of the crew shifting their opinion, and that some were starting to side with him. *Almost there*, Edwin thought, *stick with it*. Renault pondered it all with an unreadable calm as he lit his pipe and continued holding court.

"I only ever wanted my harmonica back," Edwin added for emphasis. "It was a gift from someone very special to me."

Renault shifted his stance toward Mathews with a snarl. The crew began to spread and banter, voicing their opinions and milling closer. "I might be a thief, but I'm telling you, Morris ain't no saint!" Mathews said, waving his knife around callously. "Prolly shanked Banyan in an alley somewhere or hired local yahoos to do it 'cuz he's too chicken-shit to do it himself!"

Well, damn—that's all true too, actually, Edwin thought. "Liar!" he yelled.

"You have proof of that accusation, Mathews?" Renault asked.

"I don't need proof," Mathews barked. "I know it in my gut."

"You wouldn't know your gut from your big toe, meathead!" Edwin snarled.

"Maybe I oughta open ya up a bit to settle this!" Mathews said, flexing the knife in his hand. "See if your insides are yella' or not, ay?" he added with a vacant craze, approaching steadily with the knife fixed for slicing. The crew on deck got loud and fell silent all at once…

Edwin braced for his demise…Mathews flexed the knife forward…*BLAM*—a shot rang out, leaving Mathews with a smoky bullet hole in the side of his head. He bobbled on his feet for the briefest of moments, then dropped his knife and slunk to the main deck with a gravitational thud. A flash of powder smoke cleared around Renault's revolver as he stood behind it mightily. Kersey and the crew were even more stunned than Edwin as Renault lowered his gun and strolled closer, stepping over Mathews's body to kneel in front of

Edwin with a controlled menace. "If I find out ya lied here today, the next bullet is for you," Renault said.

"You won't," Edwin said with conviction.

Renault swooped up Mathews's knife and cut Edwin loose with it. Edwin rubbed the rope burns on his wrists, unsure if this meant he was off the hook or about to get put up on a bigger one. Renault stood and addressed everyone at once. "What you men do on leave is your own goddamn business— that is, until it becomes my goddamn business," Renault said, standing above Mathews's corpse to make a point. "Now get back to your stations!"

Most crew dispersed, trying to reconcile with what had taken place. Renault motioned for Edwin to stand, and so he did. "I saw you that night, watching me," Renault said, giving Edwin a moment to deny it. Edwin didn't—he just stood there clenching his jaw. "Your conduct off duty bodes ugly on your character, Morris," Renault said. "I'm only restricting my judgment so long as your work ethic on duty remains vigorous and of substance," he added as a threat.

"Yes, sir," Edwin replied with a gulp, glancing down at Mathews's body all sprawled out and bleeding from the hole in his head, puddling under the meaty dead hand that was still gripping Lillian's harmonica. Renault glanced down as well, then scooped the harmonica up. Bits of blood ran between its chambers. Renault shook it off and placed it in his pocket.

"This seems to be a distraction," Renault said to Edwin. "Best I hold on to it until we return to Boston. Assuming you're not planning to jump ship prior?"

You smarmy old fuck, Edwin thought. "Ay, Captain. Better with you for safe-keeping, I'm sure," he said, anguished over losing the harmonica once again, after all he had just gone through to retrieve it.

"Mr. Kersey!" Renault yelled out.

"Yes, Captain?" Kersey replied, still looming nearby.

"You're the second mate now. Take Morris and those new scrubs and get Mathews off my goddamn ship," Renault said while lighting his pipe.

"Ay-ay, cap," Kersey replied, then met with Edwin over Mathews's body.

"You're welcome," Edwin said sarcastically after a brief moment of observance.

"Motherfucker, you definitely have some explaining to do, but for now, we gotta get this sack of shit into the ocean."

"Ay," Edwin said with a reluctant smirk of disbelief.

"Get us some canvas and twine. I'll go rattle the tramps up," Kersey said. He and Edwin split ways, leaving Mathews on the deck. Nobody minded. Mathews was the fourth casualty of Edwin's new beginning. The fifth, if Lillian was to be counted, and to Edwin she always was. His head rang and buzzed from Renault's gunshot for the rest of the day, but otherwise, things slipped back in to business as usual on the Salty Mariner. Edwin, Kersey, and the two crimped AB from Valparaiso, now sober enough to work and indeed familiar with the routine, wrapped up Mathews and tossed his corpse out to sea as ordered. After mopping the deck, they all took a smoke break together. Kersey was right about them, in that they would fall right in.

Price and Owens were their names, and they were indeed a pair of seasoned ocean hobos. Originally from London, they'd been traveling the world for nearly a decade, working commercial vessels and kicking around in port towns until they were out of money and got hired or crimped onto the next ship needing crew. It didn't matter where the ship was going or what it was hauling. The thought of being tied down to any one place was worse to them than syphilis, and they never kept their feet on solid ground for more than a week or two at a time. Their last run in Valparaiso was a particularly raucous leave, drinking and whoring up a tab they couldn't pay off and getting into a fight they couldn't win with the owner of the establishment. Price and Owens were not the friendliest guys on the ship, or the smartest by far, but they worked their asses off and knew the ropes. Which meant they fit right in with the Salty Mariner misfits in no time.

Edwin could sense that some of the crew still questioned his side of Mathews's story, but for the most part, relations went back to normal within a few days. Robinson got along well with Kersey as the second mate, and Murphy was soon named the third mate. CK was still making shitty coffee but the food got better for a couple of weeks after Valparaiso. When the top-shelf fare of the resupply began to dwindle down, he started keeping all the best stuff aside for Renault and the higher ups, along with a little for himself, of course. Edwin was given the duties of a boatswain some days, without title or pay increase, but remained a tried and true AB continuing to embrace the tenuous routine of his duties.

Months went by and the seas had been more than fair. The comparatively calm Pacific Ocean was nothing like the turbulence of the Atlantic Ocean they caught before turning the corner at Cape Horn. Edwin kept his head down and put in the work. He'd still meet with Kersey a few evenings per week to drink and discuss the finer things in life they couldn't have while out at sea. He also kept playing poker, and was getting damn good at it too.

Edwin had just about filled in all the pages of *The Mysterious Key* with charcoal and graphite drawings as well. Some night-watch shifts placed him up in the bird's nest of the ship on top of the main mast. There was no other sensation in the world like being up on that perch so high. Edwin felt like he could reach out and grab the stars on clear nights. It was great fodder for his drawings and provided ample time alone to ponder how quickly things had changed in the last year. Edwin thought about what the next year could bring, or the next five years, or even the next ten, if he could make it that long. He wondered how many chances he would get like the ones that had kept him moving along so far. He'd need to start controlling more of his situation, and not just being complacent with whatever direction he was being pushed. Edwin aimed to be more like the wind than to continue being the sail.

It was July now, and a cool evening chill was finally calming the hot summer day. The Salty Mariner was a week out from San Francisco, and Edwin was still debating his next steps. He wanted to jump ship but was wondering more and more if staying onboard to complete the turnaround back to Boston was the better move. From there, perhaps they'd sail to Morocco or Portugal, or further north into Europe. Parts of Edwin yearned to see the world like Price and Owens and Kersey and Lillian all had. Valparaiso had only scratched the surface of Edwin's wanderlust, but it was enough to ignite a spark. Not to mention, he'd also be a thousand dollars stronger after the payroll cleared if the run was completed, assuming he could collect without raising Wilkinson's eye. What prospects would he really have in San Francisco anyway?

Edwin toiled between the notions of staying and the rebellion and freedom of going. San Francisco might as well have been Morocco or Portugal by how reachable Edwin thought it was before Lillian's passing incited this whole mess, destroying and expanding equally his perspective of geography and morals ever since. He now faced the opportunity to see a great American city that before he'd only have been able to read about, and draw over, in a newspaper. What about making a go of it for himself—on his own terms—with nothing to lose and no attachments to bind him to any one thing or place or person or idea? What if this was a once in a lifetime opportunity? He could always fall back on being a shipman if he couldn't find employment in San Francisco, or happened to kill someone and set the crime scene on fire and need a quick escape. Plus, now he was an experienced sailor, not just some runt off the street, and would be a valued addition to any captain who was to employ him.

Renault was a manipulative, grudge-holding prick and didn't seem inclined to promote Edwin, but at the same time was intent on keeping him around, seeing as his work ethic outshined his dabble with voyeurism and accusations of wrongdoing. Why should Edwin bust his ass for no incentive, working for a drillmaster who had dirt on him, just to get fucked by Wilkinson or pinched by the brass once he got back to Boston on top of it? Because Renault had his goddamn harmonica, is why. *This old cinder-dick has me cornered*, Edwin thought.

On the morning of the day before they were to arrive in San Francisco, Edwin was in need of a plan. He stood in the galley chugging his cold, grindy coffee, then took a potato to go, gnawing on it as he walked the deck. Renault seemed busy with his mates going over preparations for the arrival, so Edwin slunk below deck and made his way to the captain's quarters. He quietly pushed the door open and stepped inside. A spicy musk of leather and booze filled the room as Edwin checked over the desk and another drawer nearby. No harmonica. He noticed a wooden chest under Renault's bed and quietly slid it out, knowing that if he got caught going through Renault's personal belongings, he'd be tossed overboard or worse. The chest was locked. *It must be in there,* he thought, sliding the chest back into place. He'd need to return with tools at the very next opportunity to present itself, ideally prior to departing from San Francisco so he could jump ship with the harmonica in tow. Edwin made sure everything he touched was back in order, then opened the door to leave—

Kersey stood in the doorway. They startled each other, then froze. "The fuck you doing?" Kersey whispered, then shoved Edwin back inside the captain's quarters and closed the door behind them.

"I don't want to lie to you, so it's best I say nothing," Edwin said.

"Goin' for that goddamn spit-box, aren't ya?" Kersey barked with a quiet intensity.

Edwin flinched. "It's mine, isn't it?"

"You'll get tossed overboard for sneaking around like this, ya fucking dummy, and they'll use me as the fucking anchor for knowing about it."

"Well, what are you doing here, then?" Edwin said, like it was a valid response.

"My job, ya dodger. Came to fetch one of the manifests, and I ain't gonna be yer fall guy if called out on seeing ya sneak, so get the fuck out!" Kersey said.

Edwin put his hands up with a pause, then said, "I won't do it again," while thinking, *I'll be back, for sure*. "We square? You won't squawk?" he asked Kersey.

"Get on, ya creep, pike it…" Kersey said, then grit his teeth and grabbed the manifest he came for from Renault's desk, pushing Edwin off. They split ways in the hallway. Kersey returned to the cockpit above them, and Edwin snaked aft to come up near the quarterdeck and start his shift like nothing had happened. They had become friendly, but Kersey was a lifer and Edwin wondered how safe his secret would be.

Today's duties were to spot-check and repair sails, and inventory the stock of materials needed for resupply while in port. Edwin slipped humbly into his work, occasionally observing Renault, Robinson, Kersey, and Murphy all at their posts as to be expected. That evening was one in the rotation that would normally be when Kersey and Edwin were to meet for a drink on deck, but tonight, Kersey didn't show up. Edwin drank by himself, hidden away from a few AB on duty, kicking back in a corner near the cockpit. He was out of paper to draw on and resorted to pondering vacantly across the water.

The next morning, Edwin kept a small kit of tools in his pocket, with an eye out for any opportunity to pillage Renault's quarters again. Morning shift went by and there was no decent window where the aft corridor was clear, which was typical, as the mates from night shift were still mulling around off duty or sleeping. Edwin saw Kersey at lunch, but they didn't speak. Kersey was busy preparing for the large cargo swap in port that he was now in charge of. It was his first port of call as a mate and he wanted to make a good impression.

During the afternoon, Edwin attempted to sneak back to the captain's quarters twice but was thwarted once by CK collecting dishes from lunch and the second time by Murphy packing a tote for his leave. Both times, Edwin didn't even get close to gaining access to Renault's corridor, and it was now getting late into the afternoon. Edwin's shift ended at dinner, and while most of the AB went to the galley, Edwin tucked back into crew quarters to clandestinely pack his duffle bag and satchel, placing them at the ready under his bunk to shove off for good. He tried again to gain access to Renault's quarters during dinner service, but most of the boatswains and mates were eating in the private bar across the way. There was no reason for Edwin to be down there, and he didn't want to push his luck with Kersey either, who was one of the men at the table.

Edwin toyed with the idea of giving up as he retired to the quarterdeck for a smoke. The sun was setting in epic fashion across the horizon line, painting the water with a sherbet luster. Edwin was not used to west coast sunsets over the ocean and was mesmerized every time. He loitered on deck with a bottle of moonshine, but an opportunity to raid Renault's quarters never presented itself. It was nearly two in the morning when the San Francisco bay became visible ahead of them. Edwin cleared the deck to allow night crew to prepare the ship for landing. He tried Renault's cabin once more while they were busy at work, but now Renault himself was occupying it. Edwin backed off immediately and returned to his own quarters. He could try again when general crew were dismissed for leave, but then he'd need to decide whether or not to go without the harmonica for good, a hard decision Edwin feared was approaching.

The Salty Mariner coasted into the wide and modern San Francisco bay under the cover of night and parked at a southern slip, leaving a long dock walk between the ship and the city. It was nearly three in the morning by the time they were secured, so instead of most crew breaking and going on leave, it was decided that leave would start the next day and that their departure would be midnight the day after. Since Edwin had leave on Valparaiso, he was assigned ship maintenance and night-watch duties through the next twenty-four hours, then would have a twelve-hour leave the day of departure. Instead of crew exiting the ship and giving Edwin free reign of it, everyone stayed on board to rest until morning leave. There was no way to sneak into Renault's cabin tonight, nor could he get away with toting his packs out in front of everyone to jump ship. Edwin decided to hunker down for the night and see what the morning could bring.

Most crew disembarked after breakfast, but there were still several men occupying the deck. Edwin joined Kersey with two mugs of coffee, and they watched several of the AB make the long walk up the dock toward the biggest city Edwin had ever seen. Even from a distance, it seemed grand and modernistic and full of busyness. Bobbing vessels of all shapes and classes lined the port. A row of shops and mills and fabricators and cafes went on for a mile, while horse-drawn carriages and dock-mounted pulley cranes got good use by hardened workers with no shortage of tasks. It was an impressive system. If the dock was this magnificent, Edwin could only imagine how frantic and imposing the city within must be. "Any good cafes, or ya only familiar with the whore houses?" Edwin asked Kersey in a manner to break the ice.

"I know a place where the steaks are as good as the zooks," Kersey replied in kind.

"Sounds hearty," Edwin said. It had been almost a year since he'd had Lillian's touch, but he still questioned how it would feel to be with another woman. He had seemingly aged five years in that time, and his urges were pulsating. He wanted to fuck, fight, and feel something, but he didn't want to just pay for it. He wanted to earn his conquests, and wrestle a fortune into submission while mounting the heads of those who would oppose him along the way.

"Getting all dreamy and lost in thought again, ay dummy?" Kersey said, as he often did to bust Edwin's chops for spacing out during their conversations.

"One of us has to do some thinking around here," Edwin said.

"Well, alright. Then I'm thinking you should probably get your ass to work." Kersey laughed, then checked his pocket watch. "I've got a supply run to rustle up and you got storage compartment swabbing to do. I'll catch ya later on."

"Ay," Edwin said as Kersey parted ways. Edwin went to work and carried out the day's duties, despite being sore about not jumping ship the night before. It would have to be tonight. Being this close to San Francisco and not being a part of it was now tearing at Edwin's convictions. He felt like it was calling his name, and he'd be damned if he'd miss this opportunity in order to mop floors and stitch patches. He'd try one more time to break into Renault's cabin just before shift change this evening, but that was going to be it. Edwin had made up his mind.

CK prepared a decent cornbread and stew dinner for the few men still on board, before he himself closed down the galley and went on leave. Edwin kept close to the aft corridor, pretending to roll a few cigarettes below deck, but Renault wasn't budging from his quarters. He was a creature of habit and rarely left his ship, having everything and anything he'd need brought to him, including meals and women. Edwin saw Robinson escorting two top-dollar comfort girls aboard, and now knew for sure that Renault would be in his quarters all night. There was no way Edwin would be able to breach that chest under the bed while Renault was busy fucking on top of it.

That made it official that if Edwin jumped ship tonight, he'd be forever leaving Lillian's harmonica behind. In that moment, the call to adventure outweighed his attachment to sentimentality. It was a heavy-hearted decision Edwin felt forced to make, but he grabbed his duffle bag and snuck off the ship. He was abandoning his post and foregoing his salary, with curious eyes leading him toward the uncertainty ahead. He felt as scared as he did free when his feet hit the dock.

"Hey, Morris!" a voice yelled out. Edwin was afraid to look, fearing a pistol or blade to be fixed on him before getting hauled back to the ship and caged. He slowly turned to find Kersey sauntering over with a bottle of liquor. "I had a feeling you'd be jumping," he said while meeting up with Edwin on the dock. "A shame, too. You weren't the biggest heap of shit we had," he added with a smirk.

"I thought about telling you," Edwin said sincerely.

"Yeah, yeah. You ain't gotta explain nothing. Just figured I'd come share one last drink with ya, at least," Kersey said, then offered his bottle to Edwin. "Got it on the supply run earlier from a local distillery. Not bad at all."

Edwin took a healthy chug. "Not bad, indeed," he said, handing the bottle back. They stood there together in silence.

"Well," Kersey finally said. "Keep your billfold tucked in tight and stay away from the opium dens. Other than that, I wish ya the best and then some, kid."

"I appreciate that. I'll miss you and our talks. Be well," Edwin said with a nod.

"Be well, Morris," Kersey replied, then turned toward the ship. "Oh…one more thing…you'll want to take this with you." Kersey held out the harmonica.

"You sneaky son of a bitch," Edwin said with disbelief as Kersey tossed it over.

"Wasn't too hard to pop that lock, but when Renault finds out, I'm sure as shit gon' let him think you did it," Kersey joked.

"Fine by me," Edwin said, shaking Kersey's hand firmly. "I can't thank you enough." Edwin stuffed the harmonica in his pocket. "I have something I'd like to give you too."

Kersey crinkled his face as Edwin fished out *The Mysterious Key* from his duffle bag. He ripped out one of the early pages, keeping a portrait of Lillian he had drawn for himself, then handed the rest of the book to Kersey. "I can't," Kersey said.

"But you will," Edwin said with insistence.

"Okay, then," Kersey replied. "You take it easy, Ed."

Edwin mugged proudly, then turned to leave. "Page twenty-two," he said with a wave as he walked off. Kersey flipped the book open and thumbed to the page. On it was an impressive caricature of Kersey's likeness. Kersey smirked and nodded proudly on his way back to the ship. Edwin moved on toward his new life in San Francisco.

To Be Continued In...

THE CRIMPER OF OLD TOWN

Part Two of the Novella Series

Scan to check out more titles available from

Loaded Image Entertainment

www.loadedimageentertainment.com/books

Printed in Great Britain
by Amazon